For several minutes Jessica stood, looking down at the grave. Then in a soft voice she began to speak to the boy she had loved.

"It's not fair," she said, reaching down to finger the wilted petals of a potted carnation. "You were too young, Sam. People our age aren't supposed to die."

A tear ran down her cheek, and Jessica wiped it away angrily. "It's Liz's fault!" she said. "Liz took you away from me!"

She clenched her fists and tried to hold on to the anger. Jessica knew that her anger was the only thing that had allowed her to get through the weeks since Sam's death. She was afraid of letting go of it. She was afraid of what might lie beneath it.

SWEET VALLEY High®

THE MORNING AFTER

Written by
Kate William

Created by
FRANCINE PASCAL

BANTAM BOOKS
NEW YORK · TORONTO · LONDON · SYDNEY · AUCKLAND

RL 6, age 12 and up

THE MORNING AFTER

A Bantam Book / July 1993

Sweet Valley High® is a registered trademark of Francine Pascal
Conceived by Francine Pascal
Produced by Daniel Weiss Associates, Inc.
33 West 17th Street
New York, NY 10011
Cover art by Joe Danisi

ISBN: 0-553-29852-6

Published simultaneously in the United States and Canada

*Bantam Books are published by Bantam Books, a division of Bantam
Doubleday Dell Publishing Group, Inc. Its trademark, consisting of the
words "Bantam Books" and the portrayal of a rooster, is Registered in
U.S. Patent and Trademark Office and in other countries. Marca
Registrada. Bantam Books, 1540 Broadway, New York, New York 10036.*

PRINTED IN THE UNITED STATES OF AMERICA

OPM   0 9 8 7 6 5 4 3 2

9/94 BM1 $3.50

Chapter 1

Sunlight glinted sharply off the surface of Secca Lake, and Elizabeth Wakefield squinted into the glare. Despite the bright sunshine, the day felt oddly cold for Southern California. Elizabeth shivered.

She usually thought of Secca Lake as a peaceful place. But that day it was more than peaceful—it was so silent that it was eerie. She listened for the soft lapping of water against the shore, for the singing of birds, and for the shouts of children playing. But all she could hear was a low humming in her ears, like the sound of a distant train.

The water was different too. It was perfectly still, and its sapphire surface seemed cold and forbidding. Elizabeth shuddered and turned away from the lake. Her gaze roamed the silent shores.

A few hundred yards away she saw a figure standing, staring at the lake. For a moment Elizabeth felt as if she had stepped out of her body and was watching herself. Despite the distance, and even though the girl's back was to her, Elizabeth knew that the girl on the shore was sixteen years old and five foot six, exactly as she herself was. Then Elizabeth laughed nervously. *Of course.* It was her identical twin sister, Jessica.

Elizabeth's long, shiny blond hair streamed out behind her like a golden flag as she ran down the beach toward her twin. Her sister's hair was tucked under a knit hat, and as Jessica turned to face her, Elizabeth noticed that the hat exactly matched the blue-green of Jessica's eyes.

Elizabeth stopped and stared. This couldn't be her twin. Jessica's eyes were usually as warm and sparkling as Elizabeth's own. This other girl's eyes were the same shade of blue-green, but they were cold and crystalline—and there was an empty expression in them that frightened Elizabeth.

"Jess?" Elizabeth called uncertainly. But as she said her twin's name she realized that the girl was not Jessica.

The girl began gliding toward her in slow, measured paces, smiling coldly. As she walked, she held her right hand behind her back.

Elizabeth's forehead beaded with perspiration. The humming in her ears escalated to a roar, as if she were standing in the path of an oncoming train. The girl who had looked like Jessica raised her left hand and whipped off the knit hat, and Elizabeth gasped. The girl had long hair the color of midnight.

Her right hand swung toward Elizabeth, and the cold sunlight flashed off a huge butcher knife.

Elizabeth tried to run, but couldn't. Her limbs seemed frozen in place as she watched the gleaming knife come closer and closer. She screamed. . . .

Elizabeth sat up in bed, gasping for breath. She pushed back the damp strands of hair that clung to her forehead. Then she held one hand, trembling, over her pounding heart.

"It's just a nightmare," she told herself aloud, trying to control her breathing. She had been having the same nightmare ever since the Jungle Prom, the night of Sam Woodruff's death.

She lay back down and curled up on her side. Tears streamed down her face and spilled onto her pillow. "Why did I ever plan that stupid dance in the first place?" she whispered.

Not long before, Elizabeth had been excited about the dance. She and Jessica were the ones who had come up with the idea for the Jungle Prom, as a benefit to raise money for saving the rain forests.

Now the whole evening seemed like a nightmare. The thought of it terrified her, though she could remember only a few fleeting images after her boyfriend, Todd Wilkins's, election as Prom King . . . the tension level rising as more students arrived from Sweet Valley's archrival, Big Mesa High School . . . she and Sam, Jessica's boyfriend, dancing while Todd posed for photos . . . she and Jessica glaring at each other across the room as ballots were handed out for Prom Queen. . . .

4

Why had it seemed so important to both of them to be chosen Queen? Why had they fought each other for the title? She was sure that the accident never would have happened if she and Jessica hadn't been competing so viciously against each other.

Elizabeth recalled how impatient Todd had been with Elizabeth's obsession to be Prom Queen. By the time she had realized that the title wasn't worth fighting Jessica for, it had been too late. Now Sam was dead, and she had lost her sister, too.

As hard as she tried, Elizabeth couldn't remember the accident that had killed her twin's boyfriend. All she knew was that she, Elizabeth, had left the dance with Sam. They had been seen together in the parking lot of Sweet Valley High School, walking toward the Jeep that the twins shared. A half hour later, police had arrived at the crash scene to find Elizabeth wandering in shock, and Sam dead.

"I killed him," she whispered. The terror of the dream was beginning to fade, only to be replaced by an even worse feeling of dread. Sam had been Jessica's boyfriend, but he was also Elizabeth's friend. Now he was dead.

Sam's funeral the day before had been one

of the worst experiences of Elizabeth's life. She hadn't been able to say a word to Sam's parents, and she had been terrified that they would say something to her. At the gravesite she had stood between her parents, grateful for their strength and protection. She was sure the Woodruffs were staring at her, were whispering that she had murdered their son. She couldn't face them, and for the entire ceremony she had remained motionless, looking down at her black pumps. The intermittent sobs of Sam's mother ripped to the very core of Elizabeth's soul.

After the ceremony, several of Elizabeth's friends, including her best friend, Enid Rollins, had tried to speak to her, but she remained rigid and stared at the ground. She knew that if she accepted anyone's sympathy, she would break down completely.

A few minutes later, she had come face-to-face with her boyfriend, Todd Wilkins. She hadn't spoken to him since the accident. He hadn't called, and she had been incapable of calling him. Her heart wrenched at the stricken look on his face, but she honestly didn't know what to say to him. Apparently Todd couldn't find the right words either. He had murmured something polite and hurried on.

As for Jessica, she had been too upset even to attend the funeral. Jessica had been one of the first people at the scene of the accident. She had been so upset that she required sedation. Elizabeth's heart went out to her sister. Jessica had a history of an infatuation with a different boy every month, but Sam had changed all that. Jessica had really loved him. And now he was gone.

Sam's death had torn a rift between the two sisters that seemed as wide as the Pacific Ocean that bordered on their usually idyllic California hometown. Elizabeth had never felt this isolated from her sister.

The identical twins had always been very close, despite occasional conflicts caused by their completely opposite personalities and interests.

Elizabeth, the older sister by four minutes, was considered the dependable one. She had rescued Jessica dozens of times from the scrapes Jessica always managed to get herself into. But Elizabeth had always known she could count on Jessica when she really needed her. Now, Jessica hadn't even spoken to her since Saturday night.

Not that I can really blame her, Elizabeth thought. *I don't deserve to be forgiven. I killed Sam. I—*

Hearing a roaring sound in the distance, she stopped abruptly and clutched her pillow in terror. For a moment Elizabeth felt that her nightmare was rushing back and overwhelming her. Then she heard the long whistle of a train and sighed in relief.

I'm turning into a real basket case, she thought, rolling over on her back and looking up at the ceiling. *A train goes by on the other side of town, and I'm practically hiding under the bed, just because it sounds like something I heard in a dream.*

She reached up and fumbled around on her bedside table until she found her reading lamp and switched it on. She knew she wouldn't go back to sleep for the rest of the night. She couldn't handle any more bad dreams.

Elizabeth took a tissue from a box on her nightstand and wiped the tears from her face. "This can't go on," she whispered. "I can't live like this."

She stared at the closed door to the bathroom that connected her room with her sister's.

She *had* to talk to Jessica, Elizabeth vowed. She had to make Jessica talk to *her*.

Sunlight streamed through Jessica's bedroom window. She opened her eyes sleepily and stretched her arms toward the light. For a moment, she imagined how pretty she must look with the rays of the sun creating highlights in her golden hair. *Sam loves the way my hair looks in the sunlight,* she thought.

Then she sat up, suddenly feeling as if she were going to throw up.

Sam.

"It's not fair," Jessica whispered. "It's just not fair." A wave of guilt swept over her at not going to Sam's funeral the day before. "Some girlfriend I am," she said. To stop herself from thinking anymore, she quickly jumped out of bed and headed for the bathroom.

Jessica pulled opened the bathroom door. For a moment she thought she was looking into a mirror. Of course, it was just Elizabeth, entering the bathroom from her own room at the same time.

For an instant the girls stared at each other

9

..hout moving. Her twin looked as if she hadn't slept in a week, Jessica saw. Elizabeth's forehead had been bruised in the accident. Now the bruise was fading, but her face was so pale that the injury looked as if it had been painted on fresh.

"Jessica—" Elizabeth began, her eyes pleading.

Jessica glared at her sister. Then without a word she spun around, stepped back into her own room, and closed the door.

She walked to her window and looked out at the lush grass and the clear, cloudless sky. Elizabeth had always said that they were lucky to live in a place as beautiful as Sweet Valley. *I don't feel very lucky,* Jessica thought, blinking back tears.

Jessica didn't want to feel sorry for her sister, but she couldn't help thinking that Elizabeth seemed to be growing more and more depressed these past few days. *She must be suffering terribly,* Jessica thought. Elizabeth had always been there when Jessica had needed her. Maybe they should be helping each other now, instead of—

Jessica bit her lip until she tasted blood. Then she shook her head resolutely.

"No," she said aloud. She didn't need Elizabeth's help. And Elizabeth didn't deserve *hers*.

Jessica clenched her fists at her sides. *Sam is dead,* she reminded herself. *And Elizabeth killed him.*

Chapter 2

The light turned red just as the black Porsche approached the intersection. Bruce Patman stopped the car and leaned against the steering wheel, a smile on his handsome face.

He was imagining a day that looked a lot like this glorious Wednesday morning. The sun was shining, the birds were singing, and he was sitting on a blanket by the shores of Secca Lake, listening to a slow jazz song on his portable CD player. He opened a bottle of the finest California cider, and then watched the most beautiful girl in the world as she expertly spread caviar on crackers.

She held a cracker out to him, but instead

of taking a bite, he put the cracker on a plate and looked into her clear blue eyes. He swept her long black hair away from her delicate face and traced the outline of her cheek with his finger. He tilted her chin up slightly and leaned forward to kiss her soft, full lips. . . .

A horn blared, and Bruce's head snapped around to look in the rearview mirror. Behind him, a bald man leaned on the horn of a red station wagon. The man's face was about the same color as his car.

"All right, all right!" Bruce said aloud. He put the car in gear and drove through the intersection. "What's your hurry, man?"

The station wagon careened past the Porsche. Normally Bruce would have floored the gas pedal and shown Mr. Station Wagon what a real car could do. But that day it didn't seem to matter. Bruce continued slowly on his way to school, still thinking of the beautiful blue-eyed girl.

Suddenly he became aware of the reggae song that was playing on the radio. It was the same song that the band had been playing at the dance Saturday, just before he and some of the other guys had left the gym to follow the Big Mesa students out to the football field.

Saturday night had been rotten in a lot of ways; Bruce hadn't even known until the next morning just how bad it was. That was when he'd heard about the car accident that Sam Woodruff and Elizabeth Wakefield had been in.

Bruce didn't know Sam very well—Sam went to Bridgewater High School, not Sweet Valley High. But he was the same age as Bruce and had always seemed like a nice-enough guy. *Sam couldn't help it*, Bruce thought, *if Jessica Wakefield had him wrapped around her little finger.* Now he was dead.

Then there was that trouble with Lila Fowler. Lila was pretty enough, Bruce admitted—beautiful, actually—but she and Bruce had never gotten along; her new-money background represented everything that the traditional Patmans hated. Her accusation against the school counselor on the night of the dance was pretty serious. Some of the kids at school seemed sympathetic toward Lila, but most were unsure exactly what to believe. Bruce suspected she had made the whole thing up; Lila had always been a tease.

Of course, Bruce had been at the dance

Saturday night when the incident had supposedly happened. But by the time the police found Lila screaming in a classroom, Bruce was already unconscious on the football field.

The fight on the football field hadn't come as any surprise to Bruce. From the moment the first group of guys from Big Mesa had arrived at the Jungle Prom, he knew that the night would end in violence. Anyone who was looking for trouble so intently was certain to find some. Physical violence wasn't usually his style, but he certainly wasn't going to back away from it, either.

For several weeks tension had been building between the two schools. A few wieners like Wilkins had tried to defuse the situation. But Bruce didn't think anybody could have prevented that fight.

He still felt a mixture of fear and exhilaration when he thought about it. It had been dark on the football field; he could barely see what was happening. Somebody hit him from behind and he fell. Suddenly a guy who was built like Mount Whitney was standing over him with a baseball bat, and Bruce was sure he was going to die.

Then *she* had saved his life.

He remembered the sound of her voice and the way her black hair glistened in the dim light from the far-off windows of the school. He remembered her big blue eyes, luminous in the darkness. But that was all he remembered.

She saved my life, he thought, touching his bruised face. *And I don't even know her name.*

He had no idea how to find her, and no experience with this sort of thing. After all, Bruce Patman had never chased a girl in his life. As the richest, best-looking senior at Sweet Valley High, he'd never had to.

Suddenly he had a vision of himself as Prince Charming, searching the town for his raven-haired Cinderella, who had disappeared before the ball was over. Then he shook his head and laughed at himself as he turned onto the street the school was on. He should just forget about her. There were dozens of girls who would give anything to go out with him. But he knew he could never forget his blue-eyed Cinderella.

Bruce drove into the school parking lot. By instinct he cut in front of Sandra Bacon's Toyota to take the last empty space in the row.

But Bruce wasn't thinking about parking spaces or cars or even school. After turning off the engine, he sat for a moment in the parking lot and leaned on the steering wheel, remembering every detail of his encounter with the beautiful, mysterious girl from Big Mesa High.

"That's it!" he said, slapping the steering wheel with his palm. Why hadn't he thought of it earlier? He would hang around Big Mesa High School every day as school let out, he decided. He would keep going back there until he found her!

After Saturday night's fight, Bruce knew that hanging out around Big Mesa could be dangerous. Guys like that brute with the baseball bat just might be the type to hold a grudge—and pulverize him.

I don't care, he decided. *I'm going to find that girl no matter what it takes. And no one's going to stop me!*

Lila Fowler slipped through the classroom door that morning and walked slowly to a desk in the back of the room. She was afraid to look up. She felt sure that everyone in her homeroom was staring at her.

After she sat down, Lila felt better, since she was less conspicuous. She shook her head slightly so that her long, light-brown hair fell around her face. Then she peeked at her classmates. They were looking away from her now, talking with each other and frantically finishing their first-period homework, as if it were any normal day.

But it wasn't a normal day. That Wednesday morning was Lila's first day back at school after the Jungle Prom. Her classmates were looking away from her on purpose; she was sure of it. They were probably too embarrassed to acknowledge her presence. *They must think I made up the whole thing,* she thought glumly.

Then she noticed her friend Amy Sutton a few rows ahead of her. Amy had turned around in her seat and was looking straight at Lila. Her expression was concerned; her eyes were questioning.

Lila tried to smile reassuringly. "I'm all right," she mouthed, answering Amy's silent question.

Amy was a good friend, but Lila found herself wishing that Jessica Wakefield was there. For the last few days, Lila had been wanting to call her best friend. Even though they bickered a lot and sometimes got on each other's nerves, Jessica could almost always make Lila laugh. Either way, talking to Jessica would take Lila's mind off her problems.

But Jessica had her own problems. Her boyfriend, Sam, was dead, and Jessica's own twin seemed to have caused the accident that killed him. As upset as Lila was now, she knew that Jessica's situation was worse.

Out of the corner of her eye, Lila saw Jean West, one of the Sweet Valley High cheerleaders, watching her from across the room. Lila noticed the expression of sympathy on Jean's face, then looked down at her hands and pretended not to have seen the petite, pretty girl. She pulled out a notebook and a pen from her oversize leather bag, intending to work on an English assignment on *Moby Dick*. Anything to keep from having to face people. But when she touched her pen to the paper, she forgot all about Melville's book.

Everybody's looking at me, she wrote quickly, without thinking. *My friends seem worried, but I don't want their sympathy. I don't need their sympathy. I just want to be left alone. The rest of the kids don't even be-*

*lieve me. I know they don't. They must think
the whole thing was my fault. After what John
Pfeiffer did to me, nobody will believe it could
happen again.*

She paused and chewed on her pen, blinking back tears. Lila had never liked to write. She had always thought that people like Elizabeth Wakefield, who wasted time writing when it wasn't even required for class, were real nerds. Elizabeth wrote for the school newspaper and actually claimed to enjoy it. But now there was nobody Lila could talk to. And she couldn't keep everything inside for much longer.

I trusted Nathan Pritchard, she wrote. *After John nearly raped me, Nathan helped me a lot. I couldn't have gotten through the last few weeks without his counseling sessions. I never thought he would try to hurt me like that.* She felt that nameless terror again, and squeezed her eyes shut for a moment, to push it out of her mind.

Maybe it was all a misunderstanding, she continued. *Or maybe the whole thing was my fault. I just don't know anymore.*

It was better not to think too much about what had happened to her on Saturday night.

Otherwise she would never make it through the day.

I wish Jessica was here, she scribbled. *Why is all this happening to us? It's so unbelievable. Elizabeth is the biggest goody-two-shoes in town, but I'm sure she was drunk at that dance. And then she drove off with* her sister's boyfriend. *Poor Sam! Poor Jessica!*

She looked up at the clock. Fifteen minutes until her first class started. She hadn't bothered to call in to get her homework assignments for the last two days, but she didn't think it would matter. Her teachers would feel sorry for her—or embarrassed about the whole situation. They probably wouldn't call on her.

The whole school seemed subdued that morning, she suddenly noticed. It had probably been this way all week, ever since the fight in the football field and the accident that had killed Sam Woodruff.

At least Jessica has someone to talk to, Lila wrote. *She can tell her mother anything. I don't even know my mother. All I've got is a housekeeper and the direct number for my father's car phone!*

Her father still didn't know about the

events of Saturday night. He had been away on business—as usual. He'd come home late Sunday, but had left the next day on yet another trip, before anyone could tell him about everything that had happened the night of the prom.

She turned to the next page of her notebook and continued writing: *My father called last night from the Chicago airport. He said his flight home would be late. He asked how I was, but he didn't really want to know. He hardly said a word to me. Why can't I have parents like my friends? Why can't I have a father who's more interested in me than in his business? Why can't I have a mother who lives here with me, instead of a mother who left when I was a baby, to live in Paris with some guy?*

The words smudged as tears fell on the page. Lila wiped her eyes with one hand and glanced around to make sure nobody had noticed.

She had told her father on the phone the night before that she was fine. As usual, he had accepted her words at face value. He hadn't cared enough to notice the tension in her voice. "That's great, honey," he had said. "Look, I've got to go. You'll be asleep by the time I get in tonight, so I'll see you . . . whenever."

He said he's bringing home a nice present for me, Lila wrote. *He's* always *bringing home a nice present for me. But he's not going to find what I really need in the shop at O'Hare Airport.*

"Lila?"

Mr. Collins's voice cut through Lila's thoughts. She slammed the notebook shut and looked up at her homeroom teacher. Mr. Collins smiled reassuringly. For once, Lila didn't even notice that he looked like a younger Robert Redford.

"Mr. Cooper would like to see you for a few minutes, Lila," he said. Lila saw for the first time that the school principal was standing next to her teacher.

Lila picked up her leather bag and her notebook. She held the notebook close to her as she slid out of her seat and walked past the rows of staring eyes. She followed Mr. Cooper out of the room.

"Is a meeting with my father really necessary, Mr. Cooper?" Lila asked quietly, staring at a cracked tile in the floor.

"Yes, Lila. I'm afraid it is," answered the principal. "As I said, we've questioned Mr. Pritchard in great detail, but we need to hear your side of the story too."

Lila bit her lip and looked off to the side. Mr. Cooper paused for a moment, watching her, then went on.

"I spoke to your father this morning," he said. "Our meeting will be held a week from today—next Wednesday at four o'clock. I would have liked to handle this situation in a timelier fashion, but your father told me he was leaving for Amsterdam today."

Lila's head snapped up. "Amsterdam?" she asked, too loudly. "I didn't know."

How typical, she thought. Her father was always rushing off on business just when she needed him the most.

Mr. Cooper looked surprised. "I assumed you knew about his trip. He offered to cancel it, of course," he said. "I'm sure he still could, if you want him to."

Lila chastised herself for having let the principal see her surprise. What was happening to her? She was used to being in control of any situation. She had to get a grip on herself.

She took a deep breath, smiled broadly, and

looked the principal in the eye. "I remember now!" she said glibly, leaning back against a locker in what she hoped was a casual manner. "He planned this trip to Amsterdam *weeks* ago. In fact, he invited me to come along. He usually asks me to, you know, but I've got this paper to write on *Moby Dick*—"

She stopped suddenly. Talking too much was just as bad as not talking at all. Mr. Cooper was watching her with a concerned expression on his face.

Lila forced herself to smile again. "Of course, he shouldn't cancel his trip to Amsterdam," she said quickly. "He has *important* business to take care of there. Next Wednesday will be fine, if that's when you'd like to meet with the two of us."

"Lila," Mr. Cooper began gently. "Along with you, your father, and myself, the meeting will include Mr. Pritchard."

Lila felt the color drain from her face as she looked up at the principal. That horrible, terrified feeling swept over her again.

Mr. Cooper put a hand on her shoulder. "Don't worry, Lila," he said. "You'll have all the help you need to get through this."

The principal turned to leave, and Lila

watched his back as he walked slowly away from her, down the deserted hallway. Then she stood, motionless, at the closed door of the classroom, afraid to open it and step inside.

The loose shutter was banging again. The noise always bothered Margo. The constant pounding had a different rhythm than the pounding in her head. She was used to both kinds of pounding, but she wished that for once they would beat together. As it was, they made her feel as if something were out of sync, as if someone were trying to confuse her.

At least the noise drowned out the sound of the Lewinsky baby screaming in the house next door. Margo hated small children. They were noisy and they smelled funny. Some people still called Margo a child, and she hated that even more. At sixteen, she was no child. She could take care of herself. She would prove that very soon.

Margo pushed her dull, jet-black hair out of her eyes and looked up at the casement window of her basement bedroom. The dirty gingham curtains were the wrong size; they didn't quite close across the filthy, cracked glass. But Margo didn't mind. Through the gap between them, she could watch the outside world without being seen.

From the ground-level window, the Long Island neighborhood looked gloomy on this overcast Friday evening. The house next door was only a few feet away. Margo eyed the long crack in its cement foundation and the peeling paint above it. Between the two houses, a broken beer bottle and part of a soaked newspaper lay in a tangle of weeds. A car rattled by in front of the house. From the sound, it was badly in need of a muffler.

Patience, said a familiar raspy whisper inside her head. *Patience.*

Then Margo heard the sound of light footsteps approaching.

"Margo!" a childish voice called from outside. "Margo!" It was her five-year-old foster sister, Nina. "Where are you, Margo?" Nina asked. The little girl sounded as if she was on the verge of tears.

Nina's thin, dirt-stained legs came into view, which was all that Margo could see of her from the ground-level window. Nina was barefoot, and Margo chuckled as the little girl nearly stepped on a glittering shard of glass from the broken bottle.

Margo supposed that Nina was all right, for a little kid. At least she was useful. Nina worshipped her sixteen-year-old foster sister. She would believe anything Margo told her, and she would do whatever Margo wanted her to do.

Margo rolled her eyes. The little girl could be awfully dense. To anyone else, it would be obvious that Margo could be found in her bedroom in the basement. She spent a lot of her time there, alone. But Margo had told Nina she would be outside that afternoon; it would never occur to the little brat that Margo might lie to her.

Margo imagined Nina wandering around the neighborhood, dodging the cars that always went too fast down Snyder Street. Nina would search for her foster sister for hours, long after it was apparent that Margo wasn't where she had said she'd be.

Margo laughed out loud after Nina disappeared around the front of the house. She liked fooling people, even five-year-olds. And she liked the idea of watching the world from this hole in the ground, where nobody could see her.

"I'm like . . . a snake . . . looking . . . at the world . . . from a hole . . . in the ground," she said slowly, in time to the beating of the loose shutter. She considered the matter for a moment before whirling around to face the bed. As a grin spread across her face, Margo announced thoughtfully, "I think I'll be a poisonous snake."

The grin disappeared an instant later, and her gray eyes turned to ice. Margo threw herself backward across the rumpled bed and stared up at the unfinished ceiling. "I hate snakes," she said, scowling as she began to twist the edge of the stained bedsheet in her fingers.

Margo hated a lot of things. She hated the cold cement floor and the cold cinder-block walls of her bedroom. She hated the piles of sour-smelling garbage bags splitting open on the curb as they waited to be picked up, through yet another garbage-collector strike. And she especially hated the iron-gray sky and the drab, boring neighborhood.

Most of all, Margo hated foster families—not that this one was any worse than the other nine she had been in. She was tired of playing the pitiful orphan, pretending to be grateful and doing what she was told. She was tired of people yelling at her and sometimes hitting her. She was tired of being told she was moody and uncooperative and just plain mean.

That's all . . . about to end, said the voice inside her head, keeping time to the pounding of the loose shutter.

Margo smiled. The last twenty dollars she had found in her foster mother's wallet had put her over the top. She now had enough for a bus ticket and some living expenses— enough to get her far away.

She was almost ready. She had been waiting for the right time for months, and it was finally here. Everything that had ever happened to her had prepared Margo for the next week. She was strong; she knew how to take care of herself. She just needed to fill in a few missing pieces of her plan.

It's too bad about Nina, she thought calmly. *She never should have walked in on me when I was counting my savings. She never should have seen the bus schedule with Cleveland circled.*

Of course, Cleveland wasn't Margo's final destination. She eventually wanted to go somewhere warm and green and beautiful. But Cleveland was far enough away so that she could wait there safely until she was ready for the next stage of her trip.

But she wouldn't be safe if Nina knew she was there, she knew. Her knuckles turned into hard white knobs as she clutched the twisted end of the bed sheet between her strong fingers. Nina would be quiet as long as Margo was there to threaten her, but once Margo was gone, she was sure that Nina would blab to everyone. Then they would probably call the Cleveland police and have her sent back. She couldn't risk that.

It can't be helped, said the secret voice.

Margo gripped the sheet so tightly that it tore.

She narrowed her cold gray eyes until they were slits. *There's nothing else I can do*, she decided. *Nina spied on me. What happens to her now is her own fault.*

Chapter 3

Elizabeth pressed her lips together and stared at the dashboard while her mother tried to make small talk.

"You'll love the plans for the new wing of the city building," Alice Wakefield was saying as she drove toward the high school. "We're going with a Spanish-style look, with lots of sunlight."

Usually Elizabeth would be interested in hearing about the latest project of her mother's interior-design firm. But today she couldn't concentrate on her mother's words.

It was Monday—Elizabeth's first day back at school since the accident and almost a week after Sam's funeral. The drive seemed interminable that morning, but at the same time, Elizabeth wished it would never end. Every block brought her closer and closer to Sweet Valley High, and Elizabeth didn't know whether she could face everyone at school.

She blinked her eyes quickly to keep from crying. This was also Jessica's first day back at school, but she had left before Elizabeth was dressed. Thinking of Jessica made Elizabeth feel even more alone.

"Usually I'm the one who's up and ready to go early," she murmured, breaking in on her mother's voice. More than anything, Elizabeth wished this was a normal morning. She longed to be standing at the bottom of the stairs of their split-level house, yelling for Jessica to hurry. She could almost hear her sister's laughter and her voice calling down, "What's the rush? The fun never starts until *I* show up!"

Elizabeth sighed. She felt as if nothing would ever be fun again. Then she saw that her mother was watching her silently, and she realized that they were in the school parking lot.

Alice Wakefield placed a hand on her

daughter's shoulder. "Liz," she said. "I know how difficult it is for you to go in there today. I want you to remember that you're not alone. Your father and I love you, honey. Your family will always be there for you."

"*Most* of my family," Elizabeth said softly.

"Jessica will come around," her mother told her. "It may take a while, but she will eventually. You know she always does."

"Not this time, Mom," Elizabeth said, looking at her hands. "Jessica can't even stand to be near me. The accident was more than a week ago, and she hasn't said a word to me. This morning she took the car Dad rented for us without even thinking about how *I'd* get to school. I almost wish she'd let loose like she usually does and tell me exactly how she feels. It might make her feel better."

"I wish she would too, Liz," said her mother. "But someday soon, she'll realize that you're not to blame for what happened."

"But what if I *am* to blame?" Elizabeth said. "I don't know how it happened, but I *killed* Sam! Maybe I don't deserve to have Jessica ever speak to me again."

"You're being too hard on yourself," Mrs. Wakefield said. She gestured toward the school. "And you don't *have* to go in there today if you're not ready—"

"No, Mom. It's OK," Elizabeth said quickly. She dabbed at her face with a tissue and then met her mother's eyes. "I can't put it off forever."

Her mother hugged her close. Then Elizabeth picked up her book bag and stepped out of the car. For a minute she longed to jump back in and beg her mother to drive her home. But going back to school would only get harder if she waited.

Elizabeth turned, waved to her mother, and tried to smile. Then she took a deep breath, walked slowly up the stairs to the school, and opened the door.

"Liz! I'm so glad to see you!" said Enid Rollins, rushing over. "I've been waiting for you."

Elizabeth took her best friend's arm gratefully and gave her a weak smile. She could always count on Enid's support. The girls pushed their way through the crowded hallway to their lockers.

"Enid, everyone's staring at me," Elizabeth whispered. "I shouldn't have come back."

"I don't think anyone's looking at you at

all," Enid said reassuringly. "If they are, it's because they're concerned about you and want to make sure you're all right."

"I wish I could believe that," Elizabeth said. Enid squeezed her hand, and Elizabeth smiled again at her friend. Good old Enid. At least her best friend hadn't deserted her—even if she was the only person who hadn't.

Elizabeth looked at Enid's sweet, round face. As long as she carefully kept her eyes on Enid, she decided, she wouldn't have to pay attention to anything else. She wouldn't have to look at the other students. She wouldn't have to see on their faces what they were thinking about her, that she was no better than a murderer.

Suddenly somebody was standing directly in front of Elizabeth. She looked up and froze. It was Todd.

Elizabeth hadn't talked to Todd since Sam's funeral. He'd acted strange that day—as if he, too, were mad at her. He hadn't called her all week, either, and she had felt too miserable to call him. Elizabeth wished desperately that she could remember more of what happened on that terrible Saturday night of the Jungle Prom. She knew she had been with

Sam that evening. Had she done something she shouldn't have? Whatever it was, it must have been awful, she thought, for Todd not to have called to see how she was doing.

Todd had always protected her when she was in trouble. Now, there in the school hallway, all she wanted to do was throw herself, crying, into his strong arms, to let him comfort her. But something in his face stopped her.

"Hi, Enid. Hi, Liz," he said quickly, not meeting her eyes. "Gotta run. I've got this math test—"

Elizabeth opened her mouth to answer, but he had slipped through the crowded hallway and was gone.

"He was angry at me even before the dance," she said quietly to Enid. "He said I was obsessed with being chosen Prom Queen. He thought I was being too competitive about it. Now I've killed Sam, and Todd hates me!"

"No, he doesn't," said Enid, her green eyes misting over. "He just needs some time to think things through. That's all."

Elizabeth shook her head helplessly. Then she pushed past her friend and ran down the hallway. A minute later she leaned on the counter in the girl's bathroom, her body racked with sobs as hot tears burned down her cheeks.

"I'm going to fail history. I know I am," Amy announced to Lila, Jessica, and Annie Whitman at lunch that day.

"You'll do fine," Lila said vacantly, tracing tiny geometric patterns on the tabletop with a pencil.

"No, I won't," Amy said. "I've got a *D* average already. Now we're halfway through the Civil War, but I can't seem to remember *any* of it. The test is next week, and I just know I'm going to fail it. My whole life is ruined!"

"I see what you mean," said Annie, a pretty sophomore who was on the cheerleading squad. "You fail one history test, and you carry the stigma with you forever. Twenty years from now, strangers will stop you on the street to ask, 'Aren't you the girl who failed Mr. Jaworski's test on the Civil War?'"

"Very funny," said Amy. "But if I fail this one, the only way I can pass this quarter is to do an extra-credit project."

"*Not* an extra-credit project!" Annie said in mock horror.

Jessica suddenly looked up. Can't you

people talk about anything *important*?" she cried.

Amy stared at her. She knew how upset Jessica was, but that was no reason for her to be rude to her friends. After all, Amy was just trying to help her get her mind off Sam.

Before Amy could protest, Jessica said, "I'm sorry. I didn't mean that."

"It's all right, Jess," Lila said gently. "Everything's going to be fine." Amy couldn't help noticing a faraway look in Lila's eyes, and she realized that Lila didn't believe a word of what she was saying.

It was tough, Amy thought, being friends with Lila and Jessica lately. Amy wanted to help cheer them up, but she didn't know how. She was used to talking with people about their problems. She was a volunteer on the Project Youth Hotline after school. But it was different when the people in trouble were your own best friends, Amy had discovered. At Project Youth, she talked to a person only once or twice. Amy had to live with Jessica's and Lila's problems every day.

She studied her friends across the table. Both looked as if they weren't getting much sleep lately. Their lunches were untouched, and Amy missed their usual high-spirited chatter.

"So are you still mad at Barry?" Annie asked Amy, breaking the strained silence.

"He's a jerk," said Amy. "He'd rather spend Saturday night watching *wrestling* on television with the guys than go to the Beach Disco with me. And then he has the nerve to say I shouldn't be mad about it. Men are so dense sometimes!"

"Men don't understand anything," Lila agreed with quiet intensity. Amy looked at her curiously, but Lila's brown eyes were absolutely expressionless.

"Speaking of men who are jerks," said Annie, "has anyone besides me noticed anything strange about Bruce Patman lately?" She gestured across the crowded cafeteria at the tall, good-looking senior. Bruce seemed to be involved in a heated argument with two juniors, Winston Egbert and Ken Matthews.

"You bet," said Amy. "He's undergone some kind of weird personality change." Neither Lila nor Jessica seemed particularly interested. "And I think I know the reason, too," Amy continued. "Here's some news about Patman to perk you two up—I know

41

you can never resist good dirt on Mr. God's Gift to Women." She looked at Lila and Jessica hopefully, but their eyes showed none of the usual anticipation. The two girls just regarded Amy politely.

Amy went on anyway. "I hear he's chasing after some girl who doesn't know he's alive," she said, laughing. "Rumor has it he's really got a thing for her."

"Who is she?" asked Jessica, looking only mildly curious. Normally, gossip like this would have sent Jessica into gleeful speculation.

"Nobody knows," Amy replied. "I don't think she even goes to this school. But it sure is making him weird—even weirder than usual, I mean. He's still the same old stuck-up Bruce that we love to hate, but now he's really manic, too. One minute he's yelling at people over nothing, and the next minute he's actually *nice*."

"Why won't he tell anyone who she is?" Lila asked.

"I don't know," said Amy. "Maybe she's a real dog, and he's afraid to admit that he's got a crush on her."

Jessica shook her head. "Not Bruce," she

said seriously. "He won't even *look* at a girl who isn't drop-dead gorgeous."

"I wish guys *wouldn't* look at girls that way," said Lila, staring at the table. Amy raised her eyebrows. Lila usually spent hours making herself look good, for the sole purpose of getting guys to notice her.

She certainly hadn't taken the trouble today, Amy thought. Lila was wearing baggy jeans and a loose cotton sweater that Amy remembered from a sale at Bibi's six months earlier. The old Lila Fowler would never be seen in last season's sweater.

"Don't look now," said Annie, interrupting Amy's thoughts, "but Mr. Manic himself is coming this way."

Bruce Patman sauntered toward them, and Amy was relieved to see that he had a smile on his face. It was bad enough, she thought, dealing with two best friends who were weirded out. She had no desire to catch Bruce in one of his new moods.

"Hello, ladies," he said, stopping beside their table. "How are you all doing today?"

He rested a hand on the back of Lila's chair, and Amy was surprised to see her friend stiffen. Of course, Lila couldn't stand Bruce,

43

but Lila was famous for usually keeping her cool.

Amy wondered again just what was going on with Lila. She knew that Lila had accused that young counselor of assaulting her at the dance. But a lot of kids thought Lila was making up the whole thing. On one hand, Amy could see why people thought she was lying. Recently Lila had accused John Pfeiffer, sports editor of *The Oracle,* of going too far on a date, of not stopping when she said no. At first a lot of people had thought Lila was exaggerating. Everybody liked John and nobody could believe he'd be guilty of such a thing. But Lila had been proven right, and John had been effectively ostracized by his peers. Still, some people couldn't believe it was happening to Lila again. Also, it was hard to believe that someone as nice as Nathan Pritchard could turn on a student like that. And even Amy had to admit that Lila wasn't above telling a few white lies occasionally, if it would help her get her way.

But Amy knew Lila well enough to know that this was different. Lila had nothing to gain by accusing Mr. Pritchard. And she seemed genuinely frightened of something.

"So, Bruce," Amy began, partly to satisfy her own curiosity, and partly to make him go away and relieve Lila's anxiety. "Are you looking for some advice to the lovelorn?"

Bruce's handsome face clouded over. "Leave it alone, Sutton," he snapped.

"Who is this mysterious girl you've got the hots for?"

"What's the matter, Amy? Are you jealous?" Bruce's cold blue eyes hardened. Then he spun around, almost knocking over an unsuspecting sophomore. Without apologizing, he stalked away.

"Wow," breathed Annie as she watched him go. "Maybe you shouldn't have said that, Amy."

"Maybe not," Amy agreed. "Though it *did* get him to leave us alone. I was only trying to embarrass him a little. I didn't know he'd get mad. If he's that touchy, it must be that his mystery girl still doesn't know he's alive, and he's really ticked off about it." She giggled. "I never thought I'd see the day when Bruce Patman made a fool of himself over a girl!"

The bell rang, and the girls began gathering up their things to go to their next classes.

"Did you hear that Lisette's is having a

45

sale, starting Wednesday?" Amy asked. "Let's go over to the mall after school that day and make an evening of it!"

"No, thanks," Jessica said slowly. "I just don't feel like it."

"I've already made plans to see a movie with Cheryl," Annie said apologetically, referring to her new stepsister.

"How about you, Lila?" Amy asked hopefully. If anything could bring a smile to her friend's face, it was a brand-new outfit, bought with her father's no-limit credit card. "After all, you are the master shopper in this crowd!"

"I can't," Lila said, not meeting Amy's eyes.

"Why not?" Amy persisted. "Do you have other plans?"

"I have a meeting," Lila murmured.

"What kind of meeting?"

"Just a meeting!" Lila answered sharply.

"OK," said Amy, subdued. "I'm sorry. We'll do it some other time."

The four girls looked at one another uncomfortably. Then they put their trays on the conveyor belt and began walking through the crowd toward the cafeteria door.

"Jess, I almost forgot," Annie said. "Would you do me a favor? I was supposed to come over to your house tonight to see Liz. She said she'd proofread my English paper for me. Would you tell her I'll be there at eight o'clock instead of seven thirty?"

For an instant, Jessica looked stricken. Then her turquoise eyes went blank. "No," she said flatly. "I won't tell her. Tell her yourself."

Annie, Lila, and Amy looked at one another in confusion as Jessica hurried away and pushed through the crowds near the door.

Chapter 4

Twenty minutes, Bruce thought later that afternoon, looking at his watch as he sat in his Porsche. *I've been here for twenty minutes today—not to mention all the time last week. Come on, Cinderella. Everyone else is getting out of school now. Where are you?*

He drummed his fingers on the steering wheel in time to the rock song on the radio.

He shook his head. Had he turned into a real space case, or what? he wondered. It was a good thing nobody from Sweet Valley High could see him now.

If anyone had told Bruce a week earlier that he'd be sitting in front of Big Mesa High

School every afternoon, waiting for a glimpse of a girl he'd never really met, he would have said that person was certifiable. He laughed at himself. How could he, Bruce Patman, be so flipped out over some girl?

"This is getting ridiculous!" he said suddenly, opening the car door. He stepped out of the Porsche, patted the hood protectively, and walked up to two girls who were passing by. Normally he wouldn't bother with girls as plain as these two—the heavyset one had thick glasses, and her friend was mousy looking. But he needed information, so he put on his most engaging grin.

"Excuse me," he began, using a tone of voice that he knew few girls could resist. "There's a girl who goes to school here. She's probably a junior or a senior—tall, with long black hair and big blue eyes. Do you know her?"

"It sounds like you may be talking about Pamela Robertson," said the fat girl. She tossed her bright red hair back in what looked like a gesture of derision. "What about her?"

"Oh, I'm just looking for her, that's all."

The girl shrugged. "Isn't everyone?" she

said. She rolled her eyes behind her thick glasses.

The mousy girl glared at him. "We don't know where she is," she said.

The two girls walked on. A minute later Bruce watched as they bent their heads together conspiratorially and then burst out laughing.

"Thanks for nothing," he said under his breath. "I never should have expected Big Mesa kids to act civilized."

They must be laughing because they recognized him as a Sweet Valley High student, he figured. *No*, he told himself. That didn't make sense. How would they know what school he went to? *They* certainly weren't the type to be crashing school dances and starting fights. Then he thought he had it figured out. They must have seen him in a tennis match—after all, what girl could forget watching *him* ace a serve?

He ran to catch up with another student, a tall, thin guy who looked as if he could give Sweet Valley High's basketball team a run for its money.

"Excuse me, but I'm trying to locate a student here. Her name is Pamela Robertson—"

The boy's laughter cut him off. "If you find her, buddy, let me know!" he said, without even slowing his pace.

What the heck is going on? Bruce wondered as he walked back toward his car. Pamela's classmates seemed awfully negative about her. Perhaps she was facing repercussions for having intervened to save Bruce's life during the fight at the Sweet Valley High dance.

That must be it, Bruce thought. He stopped for a minute, musing. What a romantic idea—a girl risking her own social status in order to save *his* life. Pamela had taken one look into his eyes and known instantly that they were meant for each other.

"Awesome car!" said a voice behind him. Bruce whirled to see a short, thin boy regarding the black Porsche. "Is it yours?"

"Oh, sure," Bruce said. He frowned. "Just be sure not to touch it—you wouldn't want to leave any fingerprints."

"Heck no!" said the boy. "When I'm old enough to get my driver's license, I'd sure like to own one of these babies."

The boy walked around the car slowly, inspecting every inch of it. "You know," he continued, "I'm a real judge of wheels. I'm surprised I haven't noticed your car in the parking lot. *This* car I'd remember." He knelt to examine a hubcap. "Of course, I'm new here," he said. "I just started two weeks ago. So I guess maybe I still don't know every car here."

He held out his hand as if he expected Bruce to shake it. "I'm Edwin," he said.

Bruce wanted to laugh, but he stopped himself. Maybe this little twit could tell him something. "Bruce," he said with a nod, shaking the boy's hand.

If Edwin was new at Big Mesa, he probably wouldn't know Pamela, Bruce reasoned. Not that a nerd would run in the same social circles as a goddess. But he might know where she hung out—his type always kept tabs on girls they could date only in their dreams.

At least, with his being new to the school, Edwin wouldn't know that Bruce wasn't a student there too.

"Hey, Edwin," Bruce said casually. "I haven't seen Pamela Robertson around lately. I know you're new here, but you couldn't miss her. Do you know where she is, by any chance?"

"Sure, I know where she is," the boy said,

still gazing at the Porsche. "I'm trying out for tennis next week, so I saw the roster," he explained.

"She's on the tennis team?" Bruce demanded. "Does that mean she's at practice?"

"Yes, she's on the team," said the boy. "She just made it last month, they say. But I've seen her play, and she really knows her stuff." He leaned toward the window of the Porsche to take a look at the dashboard. "Normally girls' varsity practices on Mondays."

"So she's at practice now?" Bruce said impatiently.

"Nope," said Edwin, still peering into the car. "The tennis team is up the coast at an exhibition match. That's why I can't try out until next week. They'll be back a week from today."

"Thanks, kid," said Bruce, unlocking the Porsche and getting in. This was too good to be true. Pamela was gorgeous, strong, and brave—*and* she played tennis! What a perfect match!

Too bad he'd have to wait a whole week to meet her.

"Hey, do you think I could have a ride in

your car?" the boy asked eagerly. "You wouldn't have to go out of your way—just take me a block or two in whatever direction you're heading!"

"Get real!" Bruce scoffed, gunning the engine.

As he pulled away from the curb, he noticed the school tennis courts nearby, empty. He gazed at the courts while he waited for a break in the traffic, and imagined Pamela Robertson's graceful figure leaping to return his perfect serve. Her glossy black hair flowed as she moved, and her blue eyes smiled encouragement at him.

"I'll be back for you, Cinderella!" he vowed. "You can count on that."

Petite, pretty Olivia Davidson stood back from her easel Tuesday evening at Forester Art School, surveying her work. She was almost finished with the watercolor landscape she was painting, a loose interpretation of the Sweet Valley Marina.

She used a dry brush to create a highlight at the crest of a wave she had just painted, smiling as the wave seemed to spring forward off the paper. Then she absentmindedly wiped the brush on her tie-dyed shirt.

"Watercolors are difficult," said a loud voice behind her. Olivia jumped, but it was only her instructor, Ms. Van Landingham.

"Watercolors tend to run and blend in ways that the artist can't always control," the teacher continued. "But this is excellent work, Olivia. You've begun with a subject, but your painting goes much further than that. It is not *about* the subject. It's about color and mood and the flow of the paint."

The art teacher turned to the rest of the class. "The trick is to allow the paint to do the work," she said. "Don't try to keep it from running. Apply it so that its natural blending becomes part of your work. Make the medium work for you."

Ms. Van Landingham moved on to help another student, and Olivia turned to root through her disorganized paint box, looking for another brush. As she did, she noticed a cute, sandy-haired boy, a year or two older than she was, watching her.

He smiled shyly as he caught her gaze. Then he blushed and turned away.

Olivia sighed, thinking about James Yates.

She had met James here at the art school, in an oil-painting class. She had been in love with him—with his honesty, his belief in his work, and his passion for painting. James had loved her, too, but his art came first. When he was offered a scholarship to study in Paris, he took it. He and Olivia had agreed to see other people, but Olivia hadn't exactly been deluged with offers.

"That's all for today, class," said Ms. Van Landingham, her voice breaking in on Olivia's thoughts. "Be sure to take a look at the paintings that have just been hung in the gallery. We have selected only the *very best* student work from throughout the school for this exhibit."

Olivia took a few steps backward again, to scrutinize her finished watercolor. Absently she ran one hand through her long, frizzy brown hair as she stared at her painting. It was as good as anything she had done so far!

Olivia was proud of the work she had been doing. It was unusual for a high-school junior to be admitted to the art school, but her portfolio had earned her the right to enroll in night classes. It still thrilled her just to be there. And as always, she couldn't get over how quickly the two-hour class sped by. Nothing had ever made her feel the way painting did—well, nothing except for James.

Olivia sighed as she began cleaning up. It was good to forget high school for a while and do something creative, something that made her feel good. But now that she was finished painting, she could feel the tension creeping back over her.

Ever since the Jungle Prom, it seemed as if the light had faded from the classrooms and hallways of Sweet Valley High. Like the rest of the junior class, Olivia had been going through the motions of attending classes and completing assignments, but her heart wasn't in it. Even the teachers seemed preoccupied. Olivia wasn't sure she could stand another depressing day of it.

"For the rest of the night, I won't even *think* about things at school," she vowed under her breath as she rinsed out her brushes. Besides, she couldn't wait to see whose paintings had made it into the student exhibit.

After putting her paints and brushes into her metal tackle box, she picked up the box by its handle and went into the gallery, which was on the same floor as her clas. As she entered the room, she noticed that several of her classmates were gathered around one work. Someone turned and saw her, and the group parted to let Olivia pass.

When she saw the painting they were admiring, Olivia gasped. It was one of her own.

"That's terrific, Olivia," said one of her classmates, a lanky guy of about twenty, wearing a paint-spattered T-shirt and cutoff jeans. His hair was pulled back into a ponytail. He tilted his head and scrutinized the work. "It's really a post-impressionist effect. The figures are indistinct, but they convey a mood. It feels almost like a carnival—but more intimate."

"Thanks, Ryan," she breathed, staring at the painting as if she'd never seen it before. Listening to people speak knowledgeably about art always made her feel alive with pleasure.

"Did you hear that you're the only one from our watercolor class to have a painting chosen for the show?" asked another classmate, an older woman named Marcia.

Olivia shook her head, dumbstruck.

The other students walked on to look at the rest of the exhibit, but Olivia remained behind, staring at her work. She tried to look at the painting through Ryan's or Marcia's eyes. She analyzed the bright, warm colors and the deceptively simple composition. She noted the way her eye was drawn to the splash of yellow in the foreground.

Nobody else would recognize the blurred figures in the painting, but Olivia suddenly remembered every detail of that perfect afternoon. She had sat under a tree, painting the group of friends who had gathered at Secca Lake for a picnic.

Not far from where Olivia had sat painting, Elizabeth sat on a large rock, holding Todd Wilkins's hand and gazing out over the crystal lake. Her blond hair, cascading past her shoulders, had shone like sunlight.

Poor Elizabeth! Olivia had seen her friend at school this week for the first time since the accident. Elizabeth was pale and listless, and Olivia wished that she knew how to help her.

I said I wouldn't think about it now, Olivia reminded herself. She put school out of her mind again and turned back to the painting.

Behind Elizabeth and Todd, a group of friends played volleyball. Olivia felt tears in her eyes as she picked out a scarlet squiggle and remembered the red bikini that Jessica Wakefield wore that day. In the painting, the figures were only splotches of color, but Olivia could clearly see two volleyball players laughing as they jumped at the same time to spike the ball.

Jessica and Sam had been so full of life that day, and so happy together. Jessica had always seemed shallow to Olivia, but even Jessica didn't deserve the awful outcome of the night of the Jungle Prom.

Olivia shook her head. She knew that if she kept thinking about what she had been looking at while she painted this watercolor, she would burst into tears right here in the hallway.

I'm an artist, she reminded herself. *I know about color and line and composition. I can appraise this painting objectively.*

Yes, she admitted. The painting really *was* good. It evoked a happy, innocent, intimate feeling. Just looking at it made her feel that she was back with her friends as they had been only a month earlier. None of them would ever be that cheerful and innocent again. Would she—and Sweet Valley High— ever be able to forget that horrible night?

"So much for being objective," she murmured under her breath.

Olivia blinked back her tears and turned away from the painting. She stopped when she noticed the cute, sandy-haired guy watching her intently from across the hall.

She held his gaze for a minute, feeling as if somehow he had guessed her jumbled thoughts. That was impossible, of course. But why was he staring at her like that? Olivia wondered. This time it was Olivia who looked away first.

Margo padded into the dark kitchen that night in her bare feet. She groped for the light switch, and the sudden brightness surprised several cockroaches. Margo watched with satisfaction as they scurried for cover.

"Scared you, didn't I?" she whispered grimly to the retreating roaches. It always felt good to know that she had power, even if it *was* only over disgusting little insects.

She checked the cracked face of the kitchen clock. It was after two in the morning. Her foster father was still out with his poker buddies—the fat ones who smoked rancid cigars and swore a lot. She shuddered at the thought of the noise and the mess they made when they were at the house. They spilled beer that she then had to clean up the next morning. It made the raggedy old carpeting smell bad. She was grateful they were playing at someone else's house that night. And after *this* week, she would never have to endure another poker night again.

Her foster mother was in bed, but Margo had seen how many drinks she'd had that night. There was no way that a little noise in the kitchen would wake her. Besides, she was used to Margo being up and around at all hours. Margo liked to prowl around the house at night, watching old movies on the late show, or just staring out the window, squinting her eyes at the street lights to make them look furry.

Margo sat down in one of the rickety kitchen chairs and leaned back until the chair touched the wall behind her. *This is the life,* she thought, crossing her arms on her chest. *All by myself, late at night, with nobody to hassle me. Too bad the TV's broken.*

Then she righted the chair quickly and jumped up, remembering why she had come upstairs in the first place. *Food.* She ran to the refrigerator and inspected its contents, holding the door open as long as she pleased.

Leftovers, leftovers, liver, moldy cheese, potatoes with stems growing out of them . . . *Yuck!* Why couldn't they ever have any real food in there?

Leaving the refrigerator door wide open, Margo sprinted to other end of the long, narrow kitchen. She jerked open the bread drawer. At least there was bread that wasn't moldy.

Toast again. Oh well, at least it was easy— that is, if the toaster would cooperate. The stupid thing never seemed to want to let go of the bread when it was finished. She placed two slices of bread in the slots and pushed down the handle.

Sure enough, the toaster began to make a screeching noise a few minutes later. "Shut up!" she demanded in a stage whisper, thinking of Nina asleep upstairs. *If that little twerp wakes up,* Margo thought, *I'll have to entertain her until she goes back upstairs. Thank goodness I won't have to put up with the brat much longer. If only I can think of a good way—*

But right then, Margo had more pressing

matters. She had to silence the toaster and get her toast out of it.

She jiggled the handle. The screeching noise stopped, but nothing else happened. Inside, the toast was turning to charcoal, but it still refused to come out. This was worse than the stupid toaster had ever acted in the past, Margo thought. She grabbed a knife and shoved it into the slot.

She jumped back as a white finger of flame shot out from the toaster and reached for her coal-black hair. "Man!" she exclaimed. "That could've set me on fire!"

Fire, said a low voice. Margo whirled around, but she knew she wouldn't see anyone behind her. The raspy voice was inside her head. *Fire,* it said again.

Suddenly Margo had a plan—a wonderful, gloriously simple, and efficient plan. It was a plan that would bring her one step closer to her goal—freedom.

The time had come.

Chapter 5

Mr. Cooper cleared his throat nervously on Wednesday afternoon. "Lila," he said, "I need you to tell us exactly what happened at the dance." He stood up, walked around the conference table, and sat on the edge of it, leaning toward Lila with an encouraging smile.

Lila looked up at the expectant faces around her. She had always considered the school principal to be kind of a jerk, but today his face was full of concern. At least *he* was paying more attention to her than her own father was.

George Fowler sat across the small table from Lila, studying his fingers. His legs were crossed, and he was tapping one foot against the leg of the table. *He can't wait for this meeting to end,* Lila thought. *He looks concerned all right—concerned about whether he'll get out of here in time to close some software deal.* She squeezed her eyes shut for a moment to keep the tears from spilling out.

"Lila?" asked Mr. Cooper.

Lila opened her eyes and shook her head wordlessly. She just couldn't talk about this—not here, not with all these men staring at her. Especially Nathan. She was aware of the counselor, sitting next to her father. Just his presence was enough to fill her with dread. But she was careful not to glance in Nathan's direction.

I trusted him, she thought. *How could he try to hurt me like that?* Lila wiped her eyes with the back of her hand and noticed that her hand was shaking.

"Lila," the principal said gently, "I know how difficult this is for you, but we have to know exactly what happened that night, from the beginning. I can ask the school nurse to come in, if you would feel more comfortable with a woman here."

Lila shook her head. "No," she said. "It

doesn't matter." She barely even knew the school nurse. There was only one person she wanted to have here with her—but her mother was probably sitting at a sidewalk café right now, looking up at the Eiffel Tower and laughing with her French boyfriend.

Then she noticed the intent, concerned expression on Mr. Cooper's face, and remembered that he was still waiting for her side of the story.

"I was at the prom the Saturday before last," she began haltingly, almost in a whisper.

"I'm sorry, honey, but could you speak up a little?" her father asked.

She glared at him. Then she swallowed, turned back to the school principal, and went on.

"At first, everything was fine. I saw Nathan—uh, Mr. Pritchard, and we talked a little bit. The Big Mesa kids started crashing the prom, and some people were worried. But Todd Wilkins calmed everyone down. Then Todd was elected Prom King. After that, everything started to get crazy."

"Crazy in what way?" her father asked sharply. Lila remembered that he had been out of town that weekend and still hadn't bothered to learn anything about the events of that horrible Saturday night.

"Well, for one thing," she explained, "Elizabeth Wakefield, of all people, was acting *possessed*. And more and more of the Big Mesa kids were around—mostly guys, but there were some girls there too. They really looked like they wanted to start trouble. They scared me."

"Did they hurt you?" her father asked quickly.

"No, nothing like that."

"What else happened, Lila?" Mr. Cooper prodded.

"I talked to Mr. Pritchard again, and then we danced, I think."

"Did he ask you to dance, or was it your idea?" her father asked her, casting a dark look in the counselor's direction.

"Um . . . It was my idea," Lila began. "No, it wasn't. No . . . I really don't remember. Is that important? We were just talking, and then we both, uh . . ." She looked from Mr. Cooper to her father, confused. "No, I think it was Mr. Pritchard who asked me to dance," she finally decided. "Yes, I think so."

Lila could feel Nathan Pritchard's eyes on

her, but she kept her gaze on her father and the principal.

"It's all right, Lila," Mr. Cooper assured her. "It doesn't matter. Just go on."

"The Big Mesa kids were showing off around Bruce and some of the other boys," said Lila. "I think the Big Mesa guys were drinking. Maybe some of the Sweet Valley kids were too. I don't know. Mr. Pritchard was a chaperon, so he went to see what was happening. Then I heard some of our guys saying they'd teach the Big Mesa guys never to show their faces in Sweet Valley again."

"And what happened next?" the principal asked.

"Everything started moving really fast," she said. "There were people all around, bumping into me. It was like a mob scene. They were rushing outside, and I was caught up in the crowd. I was scared. I was trying to get out. Then I felt someone grab my arm, and it was Mr. Pritchard."

"He grabbed your arm first?" Mr. Cooper asked. Lila thought he looked surprised.

"Yes, he grabbed my arm!" Lila insisted. Then she blushed when she realized how loudly she had spoken.

"Lila, isn't that a little different from what you told the police that night?" the principal asked gently.

"No! Uh—I don't think so," said Lila, on the verge of tears. "Maybe it was. . . . I don't remember what I told them, but I'm telling you now. *That's how it happened!* He grabbed my arm, and he pulled me out of the gym and into a classroom, and then he shut the door—"

"How dare you!" Lila's father shouted, turning to the counselor.

"Mr. Fowler, please," said the principal, raising his voice. "Let's take this one step at a time."

Mr. Fowler turned on the principal. "I cannot believe that you would allow a school employee—"

As her father argued with the principal, Lila glanced up through her lashes and saw Nathan watching her carefully. Tears shone in his eyes. Lila turned away.

"Mr. Fowler," Mr. Cooper was saying quietly, "I would really prefer to let Lila finish her story first, with a minimum of interruptions. Afterward we can discuss what actions to take, if any are warranted." He wiped his bald, glistening head with a handkerchief. "What happened next, Lila?"

Lila hesitated. "Mr. Pritchard was talking to me, I guess. . . ." she began haltingly. "But I don't remember what he was saying. No, it's just that I couldn't really hear him because of all the noise outside. There was so much noise outside. . . . People were shouting, and there were sirens."

Her voice dropped almost to a whisper. "Mr. Pritchard said something—I guess it was something about it being nice and private there. Then he put his hand on my shoulder like he was going to rip my dress, and I screamed—"

She closed her eyes and tried to stop the tears that were streaming down her face. Her father reached across the table and took her hand, but Lila pulled away from him.

"And then the police arrived?" Mr. Cooper asked quietly.

Lila nodded.

"Lila, I know how hard this is for you. Would you like to take a break before we go on to hear Mr. Pritchard's statement?" Mr. Cooper asked.

"No," she said simply. "Let's just get this over with."

The counselor looked steadily at each of

the two men and then turned his gaze to Lila. Lila stared back at him for a moment, eyes filled with tears, before looking away.

"Lila's right about events moving very quickly that night," said Mr. Pritchard. "I tried to help head off the violence, but there were too many angry teenagers and not enough chaperons to handle it. Maybe we should have seen it coming earlier." He shook his head.

"By the time the mob started rushing toward the door," he continued, "nobody could have prevented that fight. All I could do was try to keep any innocent bystanders from being hurt."

"What happened next, Nathan?" asked Mr. Cooper.

"I saw Lila caught up in it all. People were bumping into her and moving her along with the crowd. She looked frightened. I've gotten to know Lila quite well this semester. I know how vulnerable she is, and I wanted to help her. So I pushed my way through to her, grabbed her by the arm, and pulled her out of there. I took her to the nearest classroom and closed the door to shut out the confusion."

Nathan Pritchard looked at Lila. "I didn't want her to be scared," he said.

"Did you put your hand on her shoulder, as Lila says?" asked the principal.

"Absolutely not," Mr. Pritchard said. "I took a step toward her and saw a look of panic on her face. But other than grabbing her by the arm to protect her from the crowd, I never touched her."

The counselor looked as if he himself might cry at any moment. "Lila," he said, his voice shaky, "I am so sorry if you misinterpreted anything I did that night. I'm not accusing you of lying; I'm worried about you. I'm worried that being alone even with me, someone you trust, could scare you so much that you would think you were in danger. You have to know that I would never do anything to hurt you."

Lila slowly looked up to meet his gaze. Suddenly she knew that the counselor was right and that she had known it all along. Nathan had never tried to hurt her. The problem was her own, and she didn't know what to do about it.

Lila put her head in her hands and in a whisper said, "I—I made a terrible mistake. I know you wouldn't hurt me." Then she began to sob. "I'm sorry. I'm so, so sorry."

A minute later she vaguely heard her father apologizing to the counselor and the principal. But she was sobbing too hard to listen to what they were saying.

What's happening to me? she wondered. *Why am I so unhappy? Why am I making up things that aren't true?*

Her father led her out of the principal's office. Neither of them said a word on the way home.

"How about that English literature assignment?" Winston Egbert asked, sitting down on a bench beside Elizabeth the next day. He grinned. "*Moby-Dick*—is that a whale of a book, or what?"

It was lunchtime, and Elizabeth had taken her sandwich and container of apple juice outside to a bench in the school courtyard. The weather was perfect—a typical blue-and-golden California day, but Elizabeth wasn't paying much attention to her surroundings. She stared at the sandwich she held in her lap and absentmindedly pulled at the plastic wrapping on it.

She looked up. "Oh, Winston," she said. "Did you say something?"

"Nothing of any importance, as usual," he said, frowning. Winston was known as the clown of the junior class, and he usually prided himself on never getting too serious. But now he blushed and went on. "I'm sorry, Liz. I promise I'll go away if I'm sticking my nose where it doesn't belong, but you look like you can use some cheering up."

"Thanks, Win, but I'm fine," she said, elaborately folding the plastic wrap she had unwound from around her sandwich.

"No, you're not," said Winston. "You haven't been fine for a week and a half, and you know it."

Elizabeth looked at her friend and sighed. "You're right," she acknowledged. "And I appreciate your support, Winston. I really do. But right now, I would rather be alone."

"I'm not sure if that's such a good idea," Winston persisted. "Where's Enid today?"

"She has a science project."

"What about Wilkins?"

Elizabeth closed her eyes. "I wouldn't know," she said, almost in a whisper.

Winston looked down at his hands and picked at the jagged edge of a bitten-off fingernail.

Two minutes later Elizabeth jumped at the sound of another voice. "Did you see the awesome cover on the new issue of *Rock and Roll* magazine?" a girl was saying as she and her friend walked by.

The one who had spoken was short and chunky, with long blond hair. Elizabeth thought she recognized her as a sophomore, but she didn't know her name.

"Did I ever!" said the other, a tall redhead. "Jamie Peters is such a hunk! I'll just die if I can't get his new greatest-hits CD when it comes out next week."

Elizabeth studied her uneaten sandwich and waited for the girls to pass. Suddenly the redhead stopped walking and looked straight at the bench where Elizabeth and Winston were sitting. Her mouth dropped open. The blond girl pointed to Elizabeth and whispered something to her friend. As they hurried on, the redhead turned once to look over her shoulder at Elizabeth before they were out of sight.

Winston shook his head. "Idiots!" he said angrily. "Look, Elizabeth, I know you're having a crummy week. And airheads like those two don't help any. I may not be the most sensitive guy around, but if you want to talk—"

She shook her head and turned away.

"OK, I understand," he said quietly, rising from the bench. "I'll go away now. But remember that you're not alone in this, Liz. You've got friends who care about you—even if a few of them may need some more time to figure that out."

Elizabeth nodded, still looking away from him. Winston watched her for a moment, then turned and went back inside the school building. Elizabeth hoped he hadn't been able to tell that she was on the verge of tears.

Winston was right, Elizabeth admitted to herself. Many of her friends had seemed sympathetic all week. Even Mr. Collins had tried to get her to talk about the accident. As her favorite teacher and the faculty adviser of the school newspaper, *The Oracle*, Roger Collins had become a good friend of Elizabeth's and the rest of the staff. But Elizabeth didn't want to talk about the accident—not to Mr. Collins or Winston or even to Enid.

The only people I really want to talk to are Jessica and Todd, she thought. *And they won't have anything to do with me. Time isn't going to change that.*

Overhead, a sudden breeze ruffled the

leaves, with a sound that reminded Elizabeth of the distant roar she still heard every night in her terrible nightmare. The midday sun was warm, but Elizabeth shivered.

"Hey, Sis!" called Steven Wakefield as Elizabeth trudged into the kitchen Saturday morning. "Aren't you even going to welcome me back to the family homestead for the weekend?"

Steven was a freshman at the nearby state university and often came home on weekends. He reached for the maple syrup and poured some over a stack of french toast.

"Oh, hi, Steve," Elizabeth said absently. "I didn't know you were driving up this morning." She slipped into the chair next to her brother and gave him a quick hug.

Elizabeth looked across the table and tried to meet her twin's eye, but Jessica sat in stony silence, staring at her plate. Steven squeezed Elizabeth's hand under the table. But even her brother's support couldn't change the fact that everything in her life was horrible.

"Are you feeling all right, Liz?" Ned Wakefield asked from in front of the stove, where he was flipping french toast on the griddle. "You look a little pale."

"I'm fine," Elizabeth lied.

"I know just the cure," her mother said, passing her a platter. "Your father's famous french toast, with cinnamon and maple syrup."

Elizabeth obediently took the platter and picked out a single slice. Usually this was one of her favorite breakfasts, but that day she wasn't sure if she could choke down even one piece.

"Jessica, why don't you pass the sausage to your sister?" Alice Wakefield suggested.

Jessica lifted the tray and held it toward Elizabeth. As Elizabeth reached for it, their eyes met. Jessica's were icy and unforgiving. Elizabeth shuddered and looked away.

"I was flipping the channels on TV late last night, and I saw the strangest program," Mr. Wakefield began as he walked to the table with another batch of french toast. "It's a brand-new show. Has anyone heard of *Hunks*?"

"Sure, Dad," Steven answered. "It's already becoming kind of a cult thing at college. They get some poor guy as a contestant, and they set him up on blind dates with three different women. Then all four of them appear on the show, where the women rip him to shreds on national television."

"Not last night," his father said. "One of the women had very nice things to say about her date."

"Oh, that was just a fluke," said Steven, winking at his father. "You know how women are—"

He tweaked Elizabeth's nose, but she just stared at her plate, picking at her french toast with her fork. She knew her brother was trying to pull her and Jessica into a light conversation, but Elizabeth couldn't think of anything to say.

After a pause, their mother started talking about the new addition to the city building, and Elizabeth's attention drifted off again.

"And you girls don't mind clearing away the breakfast dishes, do you?" Elizabeth heard her father saying a few minutes later. "Your mother and I are heading for the garden shop to pick out a few more rosebushes."

"Fine," Elizabeth murmured. She noticed that Jessica's eyes never left her plate.

Their parents exchanged a concerned look

as they hurried from the kitchen. After they left, Steven opened his mouth as if he was going to say something, but his face fell when he saw Jessica's stony glare, and he stopped.

Again Steven squeezed Elizabeth's hand under the table. Then he stood up and sauntered out of the kitchen. As he passed Jessica, Elizabeth saw that he briefly touched her shoulder.

Elizabeth sat silently for a minute. Then she slowly raised her eyes to look at her sister. Jessica met her gaze, but her expression was forbidding.

Elizabeth swallowed hard and began in a shaky voice, "Jessica, I want to—"

Before she could say another word, Jessica leaped up from the table and bolted from the room.

Elizabeth stood slowly and began to clear the table, feeling more alone than she had ever felt before.

"Please, Margo," Nina begged, beating her palms on the sticky vinyl tablecloth, "I'm hungry! Mommy and Daddy said that *my* job was to test the front door when they left, to make sure they locked it from the outside. *Your* job is to make dinner. I did my job, but you didn't do your job!"

"They're not Mommy and Daddy," Margo snapped, standing behind her foster sister's chair, "not to you, and not to me. They're just Nasty Norma and Fat Fred Logan." She crossed her arms in front of her. "And I don't care what they said."

The little girl turned back to the table and sulked. "I'm gonna tell on you!"

"No, you won't," Margo said menacingly. She grabbed the back of her foster sister's chair and whirled it around so that the two girls were facing each other. Her eyes flashed with a hard, cold light. Nina knew not to talk back when Margo's eyes looked that way.

"OK, Margo, I won't tell," Nina said. She watched a cockroach scuttle along the base of the stove and disappear into a crack in the wall. Then she caught sight of the thickly rolled cuff of Margo's jeans and looked up curiously. "Why did you change your clothes, Margo? Those look like boy's clothes."

Margo laughed coldly, without smiling. She was wearing a loose, faded work shirt that hung down almost to her knees, over a pair of

Fred Logan's huge, greasy old jeans. She lifted the shirt to reveal an old belt that cinched the jeans at her slim waist.

"Do you like them?" she asked. "They're Fat Fred's, but he'll never miss them."

He'll never miss you, either, taunted the low, whispery voice inside her head. Margo narrowed her eyes and turned away from the little girl. *Nobody has ever missed you.*

"It's a yucky outfit," Nina decided. Then she went pale. Her foster sister's face was a mask of pure hatred.

"I was joking," Nina blurted out. "I like your outfit. Really, I do." She climbed down from the chair, turned it around to face the table, and sat down again. Then she examined the vinyl tablecloth while asking timidly, *"Now* can I have something to eat, Margo?"

Margo walked across the room, grabbed a can of soup from a cupboard, and tossed it in front of the little girl. "There, brat!" she said triumphantly. "Now don't say I didn't give you a well-balanced meal."

Nina jumped as the can hit the table. Her hands had been flat on the tabletop. If she hadn't jerked them away, the heavy can might have crushed her fingers. "But, Margo," she wailed, her brown eyes full of tears, "I'm not allowed to use the stove."

"Well, that's quite a problem, brat. I don't know how you're going to get around that one," Margo said over her shoulder as she pulled a can of kerosene from a cupboard. She had placed it there after the Logans left.

"You were nice to me today," Nina said, whimpering. "You played Legos with me. You drew Hansel and Gretel pictures for me." Tears spilled from her eyes, leaving wet tracks through the thin layer of grime on her face. "Now you're mean again. Why do you always get mean again?" She rested her head on the table and began to cry in earnest.

Suddenly Margo felt uncertain. Nina was a pest, but she was the only person who had ever seemed to care about Margo, even a little. Margo didn't play with her often, but she had indulged Nina today. After all, it would be the last time.

But did it have to be?

Margo stared thoughtfully at the back of the girl's head. Nina's life here wasn't much better than Margo's—except that she was still little, so people thought she was cute. Margo knew that Nina had no family either, except for a grown brother in New Jersey who worked weird hours and supported his dead wife's sick mother.

For a split second Margo seriously considered taking her foster sister along with her.

Nina's slim shoulders trembled as she sobbed quietly into her arms. Margo stared at the fragile nape of her neck. The little girl's dirty blond hair never would stay in a ponytail. A few tendrils had pulled out now; they bobbed limply as she sobbed. Nina looked so vulnerable, Margo thought.

And so weak, whispered the raspy voice in her mind.

A wave of disgust washed over her. Margo hated weakness.

"Stop behaving like a child!" she yelled at the girl. She whirled to face the counter again, and opened the can of kerosene.

Nina stuck out her bottom lip in a pout. "I'm hungry, and I want dinner!" she whined, turning around in her chair to make sure that Margo could see how much she was suffering. Then her expression changed.

"Wait, Margo—you spilled that stuff all over the place!"

Margo threw her hands up in mock surprise. "Silly me!" she said. "I sloshed kerosene all over the nice clean counter! Whatever will the maid think of me?"

"I won't tell on you for spilling it, if you'll make me something to eat," Nina promised solemnly.

"You know what, brat?" said `Margo. "You're really beginning to annoy me." She grabbed a loaf of bread and hurled it at the table. "Here, crybaby," she said. "Stick a piece of toast in the toaster. Think you can handle that?"

She laughed cruelly and skipped downstairs to her room.

A minute later, Margo picked up an old baseball cap of Mr. Logan's. She stood in front of the cracked mirror, put the cap on her head, and tucked her dark hair into it.

"There," she said to her reflection. "I'm a new person already."

She grabbed her packed duffel bag. Then she stopped for a minute to look around at the cold cinder-block walls, the unmade bed, and the ugly, dirty, too-small curtains. "Good-bye, grungy basement—and good riddance!"

Margo took the stairs two at a time, making sure to step in time to the familiar pounding that was starting up again in her head.

She stopped at the back door and looked into the kitchen. Nina was standing on a chair, peering into the toaster. She heard Margo and turned around. Margo saw with amusement that Nina had tears in her eyes and that she was sucking on the fingers of one grimy hand.

Nina held up two reddened fingers. "I burned myself, Margo. Will you help me, *pleeease*? The bread is stuck, and I can't get it out!"

"You idiot," said Margo, shaking her head. "Do I have to do everything for you? Anyone with half a brain would know to dig it out with a butter knife."

"OK," Nina said with a smile. Then she slid off the chair and reached for the silverware drawer.

Margo opened the back door and stepped outside into the dark, cool night. She watched through the window as Nina, knife in hand, climbed awkwardly back onto the chair. Margo locked the door from the outside. Then she noticed that Nina had turned again and was staring at her through the window in consternation.

"Margo, where are you going?" the little

girl cried through the window, which was open just a few inches. "You're not supposed to leave me here alone. Mommy and Daddy said—"

Without a word, Margo strode away from the house.

"They're not our Mommy and Daddy," she said fervently.

Orange flames whirled against the dark sky. They reminded Margo of the violent stars in a Van Gogh painting an art teacher had shown her once, at one of the many schools she had attended.

Margo was standing on Snyder Street, a block away from the Logans' house, edging her way into a crowd of people.

"I saw them take out one body," an elderly woman was saying. In the wavering glow of firelight, Margo recognized her as the blue-haired lady from the boardinghouse across the street—Old Blue Hair, Margo had always called her.

Margo turned her face away, just in case. But between the dark night and the men's clothes she wore, she didn't think anyone would recognize her. A family with about a zillion kids had recently moved in up the street. Surely everyone would assume she was one of that brood.

"There was a sheet over the body, so I couldn't tell for certain," said the blue-haired woman. "But it had to be the little brown-eyed girl. It was too small to be the other one."

"Where are the parents?" asked a middle-aged man.

"The Logans drove away late in the afternoon," said Margo's next-door neighbor, Mrs. Lewinsky. "I don't know where they went."

The man shook his head. "The Social Services people aren't going to like this—not one bit. I heard the fire chief say that both doors were locked from the outside!"

"I'm certainly not surprised," said Old Blue Hair. "They neglected those foster children. The little girl was always running around the neighborhood like a stray cat, and that teenager—"

"A real weird one, she was," Mrs. Lewinsky agreed, shuddering. "Always seemed to look right through you with those big gray eyes."

Margo felt triumphant, but strangely sad. She was finally going away, but nobody would miss her. How could they? Nobody had ever bothered to get to know her. Not in this neighborhood and not in any of the other neighborhoods she had lived in.

"It's a shame about the children—even if the older one *was* a sullen, disagreeable girl," said the man, wiping the sweat from his forehead.

"You know," Mrs. Lewinsky began, "in all the time she lived next door, that girl hardly ever said a word to me. Why, I'm not even sure of her name. What was it—Marla? Margaret?"

"Michelle," Margo said suddenly, coming to a decision. Then she saw the three adults staring at her, and she realized she had spoken out loud.

In the dim orange glow, Margo saw herself reflected six times in their eyes. For a moment she wondered who that dirty-looking boy was. Then she turned away and pretended to be admiring the fire engines. That was the kind of thing people expected boys to like, wasn't it?

"No, that's not right," Old Blue Hair said. "I'm sure her name wasn't Michelle, but I can't for the life of me remember—"

"She may still be alive," said Mrs. Lewinsky. "They haven't found a second body yet. But there's no way they'll save that house. I'm just thankful they were able to keep the blaze from spreading."

"Oh, the teenager's dead all right," said the man. "Feel the heat from that fire. Nobody could've lived through it."

"Margo!" exclaimed Old Blue Hair. Margo jumped, frightened. "Her name was Margo."

"Not anymore," Margo mumbled. Suddenly she felt as if the fire were in her head.

Keep moving, said the voice in her head.

Margo left the group and stumbled toward the fire engines. *There is no Margo anymore,* she thought as she walked faster, in step with the throbbing in her head. What a headache! Probably the smoke was getting to her. She shook her head as if to rid it of unpleasant memories.

"Margo is dead," she said, narrowing her blue eyes. *"I am Michelle."*

It was time. Margo took one last look at the orange flames that swirled against the night sky. Then she turned her back on the smoke-filled neighborhood and ran.

Chapter 6

Olivia strolled along the sun-dappled sidewalk in downtown Sweet Valley, swinging her paint box in one hand and her book bag in the other. She stopped in front of a pet store, where a cocker spaniel puppy eyed her playfully from the shop window.

"I bet I'm the happiest girl in Sweet Valley!" she told the puppy. Then she sighed, remembering. Of course, that wasn't saying a lot, lately.

It was Monday afternoon, more than two weeks after the prom, but the atmosphere at school hadn't improved. Depression still hung like fog in the hallways of Sweet Valley High.

Olivia had never been so glad when the last bell rang and school was finally over for the day.

She had taken the bus downtown to run some errands. Now the afternoon sun painted long shadows on the bright pavement, a few fluffy clouds moved lazily overhead, and the cocker spaniel gazed at her worshipfully from the pet-shop window.

Olivia leaned forward to smile at the eager puppy. "Another adoring fan!" she said with a dreamy sigh.

She tossed her head to shake her frizzy brown hair out of her eyes. Then she stared through the pet-shop window until the wire cages inside the store were transformed into rows of seats where elegant, artsy people perched as they strained to hear the auctioneer. This was Sotheby's—the famous art auction house.

The crowd commented excitedly as the latest masterpiece by Olivia Davidson was placed on the auction block.

"Four million!" barked a thin, long-nosed man in a sleek gray suit.

"Five million!" said a beautiful, sophisticated woman in a simpe but elegant red silk dress.

"Six million!" said the long-nosed man.

"Seven!" responded the woman.

Suddenly a well-built man with shaggy red hair stood up in the back of the room. Olivia noted his heavy Irish accent as he growled, "I bid ten million dollars."

"Olivia, you look like a million bucks!" came a voice.

Olivia whirled around. Nicholas Morrow had just crossed the street to join her.

"I mean it," he said, pushing a lock of dark wavy hair out of his eyes. "I haven't seen anyone in town look so happy in weeks! What's up?"

"Hey, Nicholas!" Olivia said, smiling broadly. She turned to wink at the cocker spaniel, then fell in step beside her friend as he began walking.

"I *am* happy," she admitted. "Actually, I've been dying to tell someone my news for the last two hours, but I just couldn't. Everyone at school is so down that I felt guilty about being happy."

"Things must be pretty rough at school," Nicholas said seriously, with just a hint of a Boston accent. "I'm glad I graduated last year so I don't have to be there. It's terrible to lose someone who was so young."

Nicholas turned his head away for an instant, but not before Olivia saw a flash of pain in his green eyes. She knew he was thinking of his sister, Regina, who had died some months earlier, at age sixteen.

After a moment Nicholas looked back at Olivia and grinned. "So how big is this big news of yours? Big enough for a celebration?"

"Absolutely!" Olivia said. "But Nicholas, it's only four o'clock. I thought only we carefree high-school kids got out at such a civilized hour. Aren't you supposed to be at work for your father?"

"Nope," said Nicholas. "I'm a free man as of half an hour ago! I was in the office at a horrendous hour this morning, so my dad said I could take off early."

"In that case, I'd love to celebrate!" Olivia said. "What did you have in mind?"

"There's a new place on the next block that I've been meaning to try—Café Feliz. We can sit at an outdoor table under a striped umbrella and eat something decadent—my treat—while you tell me your news!"

"So what are we celebrating?" Nicholas

asked Olivia at Café Feliz a few minutes later, after they had given their orders to the waiter. "I can't stand the suspense any longer!"

"You know that I've been taking a water-color class at the Forester Art School," Olivia began. "Well, one of my paintings was chosen last week to be in the big student art exhibit—"

"Congratulations," said Nicholas. "That's terrific, Olivia."

"Thanks," she said. "But there's more. Today the art school sent word through my art teacher at high school that somebody wants to buy my painting!"

"All right!" Nicholas exclaimed. He gave a thumbs-up signal and then leaned over the white plastic table to give her a brotherly peck on the cheek. "So who's the lucky art collector?"

Olivia shrugged her shoulders. "I have no idea. They haven't told me his name. But get this—the guy has offered *one thousand dollars* for my painting!"

She couldn't help noticing the waiter's impressed stare as he set their desserts on the table.

"I almost fainted when Mr. Traviano at school told me," Olivia continued after the waiter had left. "In fact, I thought someone had made a mistake and added an extra zero! I can still hardly believe it."

Nicholas saluted her with a spoonful of banana split. "Well, I can!" he said. "You've got real talent. It's about time the rest of the world started noticing it!"

Olivia sipped her cappuccino. "There *is* one condition," she said. "The collector wants me to give a talk about my work this week at a fund-raiser at a place called the Coastal California Fine Arts Foundation. It's somewhere in Bridgewater."

"That's great, Olivia. It sounds like your career is taking off in a big way. Are you nervous about speaking?"

Olivia nodded. "Petrified," she said. "It's awfully short notice, and I don't have much experience with public speaking. But it's great exposure, and it's a small price to pay to make my first big-time sale!"

Nicholas raised his ginger ale in a toast. "Look out, Picasso!" he said. "I can see it now. Within a few years, your work will be going for millions of dollars, and every art critic in the country will be raving about it."

Olivia blushed, remembering her daydream. She picked up her fork and started in on her carrot cake. "Well, I don't think I'm quite ready for a major New York gallery!"

"I just hope you have a more exciting celebration than *this* planned for tonight," Nicholas said, gesturing around them. "Something a little more—romantic?"

"I thought I'd curl up on the couch with Kirk Douglas!" Olivia said. "Actually, I've rented his old movie, *Lust for Life,* about Vincent Van Gogh."

Nicholas rolled his eyes. "Van Gogh? Great. He painted twenty-five hours a day, sold a grand total of one painting in his whole life, and then, just for fun, cut off his ear before he committed suicide. Well, that ought to be good for a few *laughs.*"

Olivia smiled at Nicholas's reaction. "But I like movies about artists."

Nicholas shook his head. "Do you mean to tell me that none of the guys at Sweet Valley High has had the sense to try to sweep you off your feet, now that James is out of the picture?"

"This morning the janitor nearly knocked me over with his broom," Olivia said, laughing. "Does that count?" She scooped up some cream-cheese frosting on her fork and licked it off. "Seriously," she continued, "I haven't had a single date since James moved to Paris."

"You really miss him, don't you?"

Olivia nodded. "Yes, but I couldn't ask him to give up his chance to study art in France, and both of us hated the idea of a long-distance relationship."

She was silent for a minute. "I know we made the right choice when we decided to see other people. But lately I find myself thinking that even a long-distance relationship might be better than no relationship at all."

"Do you really mean that?"

Olivia was thoughtful for a moment. "No, I guess not," she finally said. "It never could have worked out; we're just too far apart now. And James has to be able to concentrate exclusively on his painting."

She paused. "It's not that I'm *desperate* or anything, Nicholas. I know I don't have to have a boyfriend to be a complete person. Still, it would be nice to have a date now and then."

Nicholas sighed. "That's for sure," he agreed.

"So you're still playing the field, since you and Andrea Slade broke up?"

"Playing the field and dropping every ball," he said ruefully. "Give it to me straight, Olivia. Am I using the wrong after-shave? Are my socks the wrong color? Maybe I should grow a beard. Tell me—*what do women want?*"

"If *you're* not it, Nicholas, I don't know what is," said Olivia. She began counting off on her fingers. "You're tall, dark, and handsome. You're smart and fun. You have a great personality. And you own a sailboat." She threw up her hands. "Face it, you're perfect in every way. There's obviously something wrong with the girls in this town."

"You don't have a twin sister I don't know about, do you?"

"Sorry, Nicholas! And I can't think of anyone at school who's good enough for you, except for some of the girls who already have boyfriends. But there's got to be a way to help you find a girlfriend. Give me time. I'll think of something."

"My love life is in your hands," said Nicholas, grinning. "OK, that solves *my* romantic problems. Now let's get back to work on yours."

Olivia set down her fork and leaned back in her chair. "No," she said. "The only time I ever seem to find a good relationship is when I'm not looking for one. I just need to stop moping around, wishing for the perfect boyfriend to drop out of the clouds."

Nicholas shielded his head with his arms and scanned the sky, an exaggerated look of concern on his face.

"I didn't mean that literally," Olivia said, and laughed. "My other choice is to resign myself to being single for the rest of my life. Then I can put all my energy into my painting and my writing."

"You're a little young to be worrying about being single for the rest of your life," Nicholas objected.

Olivia laughed. "That may have been a *slight* exaggeration," she admitted. "We artists tend to be overly dramatic when it comes to love."

Nicholas grinned. "Just make sure you call me if you get an urge to cut off your ear!"

Bruce whistled. *Poetry in motion*, he thought. *Absolute perfection.*

Pamela's shapely arm arced through the air as she executed a perfect serve. Her opponent missed the return by a mile, and Bruce realized that Pamela's easy grace was deceiving. Her serve was nearly as powerful as his own.

He was impressed, but not surprised. Of course she was stunningly beautiful and had a terrific figure. Of course she was a fabulous tennis player. Pamela was perfect—the girl of his dreams. Nothing could make Bruce happier than being near her, watching her graceful movements and feeling the warmth of her smile.

Well, there was one thing that would make him happier, he reminded himself. He still hadn't met her. Well, not really.

What if she didn't remember him? he wondered, drumming his fingers nervously on the steering wheel of his black Porsche. What if she didn't *like* him?

He considered the possibility in horror for a minute, then dismissed it with a wave. That couldn't happen; they were made for each other.

He leaned back in the driver's seat, impatient with himself. He was beginning to act like a complete dweeb, head-over-Nikes in love with a girl he'd never spoken to!

But Bruce couldn't help himself. He had never seen a girl who looked sweeter than Pamela Robertson, and he was determined to ask her out.

He got out of the Porsche and sauntered over to the tennis court to watch the end of the match.

"Awesome game, Lisa!" said Pamela, reaching for her towel. "You had me worried toward the end there."

"No, I didn't," said her tall, auburn-haired friend. "You're just being polite. You beat me easily, like you always do."

Bruce, standing at the edge of the court, sighed. Pamela was modest and compassionate, as well as beautiful and brave. The girls walked past him toward the school, and he rushed to catch up.

"Pamela!" he said.

She turned toward him, and Bruce marveled at the way the sunlight caught the blue-black highlights in her hair as it swung around her lovely face. She looked a little uncertain, but friendly.

"I'll catch you later, Pam," said Lisa. Bruce

noticed the sly wink she gave Pamela before she walked off, swinging her racket by her side. He wondered briefly what the wink was for, but then Pamela was standing right in front of him, and Bruce forgot everything else.

"I—I don't know if you remember me," he stammered, surprised at how nervous he suddenly felt. "I'm Bruce Patman, the guy whose life you saved the night of the Sweet Valley High dance."

Pamela gave a musical laugh. "Of course!" she said. "I didn't recognize you in the daylight. I'm really sorry about all that—"

Bruce interrupted. "Don't be," he said. "It wasn't your fault. Those guys were animals."

"I see the cut on your face healed," she said. She raised her hand to within a few inches of his cheek, and Bruce felt something like an electric current jump from her fingers to his face. His whole body tingled, and he wondered if she had felt it too.

Pamela's blue eyes widened. She dropped her hand slowly, and smiled.

Bruce looked into her eyes. He wanted to wrap his arms around her slender figure and kiss her, right there by the tennis courts. "I'd like to repay you for what you did that night," he began instead. "I was wondering if you'd like to have dinner with me tomorrow night—"

"I'd love to!"

Pamela gave Bruce her address, and he arranged to pick her up at seven the next evening. With a big smile and a wave, she said good-bye, then headed toward the street.

As Bruce walked toward the Porsche, he felt like jumping into the air and clicking his heels together. In just twenty-four hours, he would be getting ready for his first date with his dream girl.

It appeared as though the night of the Jungle Prom was turning out to be the luckiest night of Bruce Patman's life.

"I tried talking to Todd again this afternoon," Enid said that evening, sitting cross-legged on Elizabeth's rumpled bed.

"Did he tell you anything?" Elizabeth asked quickly, her eyes wide.

"No, I'm sorry," Enid said, shaking her head. "He won't talk to me, either."

Elizabeth was sitting backward in her desk chair, facing Enid. Enid noticed a stack of notebooks that had fallen over on the desk behind her. If it had been anyone else's desk, especially her own, Enid wouldn't even have noticed the disarray. But Elizabeth's was usually immaculate. Now, the desk was a mess, and Elizabeth's bed was unmade. This uncharacteristic sloppiness worried Enid.

But worst of all was the pain and confusion Enid saw on Elizabeth's face.

"I just wish I knew *why*," Elizabeth said. "Todd's angry at me for *something* I did that night, and I don't remember it! Enid, what could I have done that was so terrible?"

"I doubt you did anything at all, Liz. I think this whole thing has been hard on him, too. He may be having a hard time handling Sam's death. Also, he was probably upset that you left with Sam. Or maybe he just misinterpreted what he saw."

"But what could he have seen?"

Enid opened her mouth to speak. Then she closed it and shook her head. It was no use repeating rumors. That would just upset her friend even more.

"Enid, you heard something at school, didn't you?" Elizabeth asked, seeing the hesitant expression on her best friend's face.

"Please, you've got to tell me."

"Elizabeth, it's just a rumor. It's probably got no basis in truth at all."

"What's just a rumor?"

Enid took a deep breath. "Caroline Pearce told me that somebody saw you with your arms around Sam Woodruff during the prom. She made it sound like you were hugging him—and not just a friend-type hug."

Elizabeth's mouth dropped open, and she stared at Enid. "What?"

"Look," Enid said, "you know how Caroline exaggerates. You were dancing with Sam, so of *course* you had your arms around him! Anyway, it's just a rumor," she said again. "You know how rumors grow."

Elizabeth took a deep breath. "I remember dancing with Sam," she said haltingly. "But hugging him? Why would I hug my sister's boyfriend?"

"I don't know. Maybe the whole thing is a lie. Or maybe somebody saw some other blond girl hugging a guy and thought it was you. Or maybe you were just giving Sam a friendly hug. You know how people talk."

"Yes, and they must be talking a lot," Elizabeth said. "It seems like every time I walk

110

into a room at school, conversation stops. Nobody will tell me anything to my face. They're still saying I was drinking, aren't they?"

Enid hesitated. "Yes," she said finally.

"Well, that's one rumor that seems to be grounded in fact," Elizabeth said. Her voice dropped so low that Enid had to lean forward to catch her words. "Why else would I not remember anything?" Elizabeth asked. "I don't understand it. The only thing I drank that night was punch, and it was from the same punch bowl that everyone else was drinking from! It wasn't spiked or anything."

"I'm sorry, Liz. I should have been paying more attention to what was happening with you that night. I was caught in the cross fire of all that school-rivalry stuff, with the Sweet Valley guys harassing Hugh just because he goes to Big Mesa—"

"Don't blame yourself, Enid," Elizabeth protested. "You had your hands full, with a boyfriend from the rival school. Besides, I don't need anyone to baby-sit me."

Elizabeth stopped and bit her lip. Then she took a deep breath and stared intently at her friend. "Enid," she continued, "no matter what happens, I want you to know how lucky I feel to have you for a friend. I don't know what I'd do without you—especially now that Todd hates me, and Jessica—" She shook her head, unable to go on.

"I'm worried about you, Liz," said Enid, with tears in her eyes. "I've never seen you acting this way. You seem so alone and depressed, and I don't know how to help you."

"You do help me. You help me more than anyone." Elizabeth's voice sank to a whisper. "But I don't know what to do, Enid. I can't sleep at night without having horrible dreams. Then I sit down and try to write in my journal, but I can't think of anything to write. Usually I have so much to write that I have trouble keeping up."

Enid felt her own fear growing. Elizabeth could *always* write about what was bothering her; it was the best therapy for her when she was upset. For Elizabeth, losing the ability to write was almost as devastating as losing her sister.

Suddenly Enid realized how dark the room had become. She switched on the reading lamp. "Have you talked to your parents?" she asked.

"A little bit," said Elizabeth. "They're trying to be supportive, but they seem lost, somehow. And Jessica hardly says a word to anyone." She stared at her hands for a moment before continuing. "The four of us have been walking around this house like ghosts," she said in a lifeless voice. "The only time it's even a little bit more normal is when Steven's here, but he's only here on weekends, and then not every weekend."

She thought for a minute. "I don't know, Enid," she said finally. "It's all so unreal, like a dream that you can't wake up from."

"Have you tried to talk to Jessica lately?" Enid asked.

"Not since breakfast Saturday morning. And I told you how much good *that* did. I've got to face it—Jessica's never going to speak to me again."

"Jessica's been through a lot in the last few weeks," Enid said. "It will take time, Elizabeth, but she'll come around, and so will Todd. He'll remember how much he loves you, and Jessica will realize that she can't go on blaming you—"

"*But I am to blame!*" Elizabeth shouted. "*It was my fault!*"

Enid took her friend's hand. "No, Elizabeth. You can't do this to yourself. It was an accident, a terrible accident."

Elizabeth yanked her hand away. "Don't you see?" she said. "I killed Sam! I killed him!"

Enid stood up and tried to hug her, but Elizabeth pulled away. She jumped up and walked across the room.

"Liz—"

Elizabeth stood staring out the window at the darkening sky. Her slim back was perfectly still, and she looked thinner and more vulnerable than Enid had ever seen her.

"There are legal repercussions in a case like this," Elizabeth said levelly. "I might as well prepare myself for the worst."

"Liz, I don't think you have anything to worry about. The police could tell that it was an accident. You don't even know for sure if you were the one who was driving the car!"

Elizabeth turned and stared at her friend, and Enid saw an eerie coldness in her blue eyes.

"You still don't get it, Enid," Elizabeth said. "I did it, Enid. *I am guilty.* Sooner or later, the authorities are going to realize it too."

Chapter 7

The phone had been ringing for some time, but Lila barely noticed it. She was sitting at her bedroom window, staring out at the swimming pool that shimmered in the near-darkness.

"Lila!" came her father's voice from downstairs. "That's your personal line. Are you going to pick it up?" She heard him come partway up the stairs. "Are you all right, honey?" he asked.

For almost a week, Lila had been ignoring the phone whenever it rang. She just didn't feel like talking to people. No, it was more than that. She was *afraid* to talk to people. The whole world probably knew by now what she had wrongly accused Nathan Pritchard of, and she didn't know what she would say if anyone asked her about it. But it was more than that. She was just afraid, period. Lately, being around people at all—especially boys or men—made her pulse race and her forehead break out in a cold sweat.

But her father was beginning to sound worried. He hadn't appeared to believe her on Friday when she told him she would be studying all weekend, but at least he hadn't questioned her any further. Lila hadn't opened a single book since then. She had been alone in her room since Friday afternoon; by now her father must know that something was really wrong.

He would probably try to talk to her again soon, Lila thought. And the last thing she wanted was a heart-to-heart talk with her father. Maybe he would be less worried about her if she took this phone call, as if everything were normal.

Lila stared at her phone for a few seconds longer, then lifted the receiver.

"Yes?"

"Lila?" asked a voice. "Where have you been? Are you all right?"

For a moment, Lila felt as if she were asleep and couldn't quite wake up. Then she recognized the voice as Amy's. She noticed, in a detached kind of way, that Amy's voice was full of concern.

"Hi, Amy. I'm fine," Lila said. Her voice was listless, but she gripped the receiver so tightly that her knuckles turned white.

"You weren't in school most of last week, and I tried calling you all weekend. When you were out of school again today, I really got worried. What's wrong?"

"Nothing," Lila said.

"What do you mean, *nothing*? How could you be out of school almost a whole week for no reason at all?"

"A week? What day is it?"

"It's Monday, of course! What's the matter, Lila? Were you asleep when I called?"

"Asleep?" Lila asked, feeling stupid. Her brain seemed to be made of hair mousse. "No," she said finally. "I haven't been able to sleep all week."

"Lila, I'm worried about you. What's wrong?"

"It's the flu," Lila said quickly. "That's it—just the flu."

She heard Amy sigh in relief. "Well, I'm glad it's nothing more serious. But I thought you said you were fine."

"Did I?" asked Lila. "I meant that I'm a lot better than I was last week. But I still have the flu."

"You're going to be so far behind in history that it'll take you until graduation to catch up," Amy warned. "Mr. Jaworski expects us to know absolutely everything about the Civil War by Wednesday. I just know I'm going to have to do an extra-credit project to pull my grade up after that. I was thinking of doing a genealogy project—you know, trace my family tree. Actually, it was my mother's idea. . . ."

As Amy spoke, Lila stared at her reflection in the mirror. She fingered the hollows in her cheeks and the dark circles beneath her eyes. Her long, light-brown hair, usually lustrous and perfectly groomed, hung limply around her face. She wondered why it looked so bad, then realized that it had been days since she had washed it. She had just forgotten to. And now it didn't seem to matter.

I do look sick, Lila thought, still appraising her image in the mirror. In fact, she looked ugly—worse than she had ever looked in her whole life. But Lila didn't care. There was nobody here to see her, and she had no intention of leaving her room.

Suddenly Lila realized that Amy had stopped talking and was waiting for her to say something.

"Uh—I'm sorry, Amy," she stammered. "What did you say?"

"You really are a space cadet!" Amy said with a tentative laugh. "I said that I could bring my books over tomorrow night and we could study for the Civil War test together."

"No, I don't think so."

"It's no trouble, Lila. Besides, if I really have to study, I'd rather do it at your house than mine. Since my mother's been on a diet, there's nothing but celery in the refrigerator. I can come over right after cheerleading practice."

"Don't," Lila said, a little too sharply. "I mean, uh, I don't think I'll be feeling well enough by then to see anyone."

"Are you sure, Lila? I mean, you sound like you could use some cheering up."

119

"I'm sure, Amy."

Amy hesitated for a minute. "Lila, please tell me what's going on!"

"Nothing's going on," Lila insisted, forcing a laugh. "Nothing at all is going on except for the same old boring rut," she said. "Oh, I think I hear my father calling me. I've got to run, Amy. Bye."

A few minutes later, Lila really did hear her father's muffled footsteps on the thick carpeting of the hallway.

He tapped on the door. "Lila?" he called softly. "Can I come in?"

"I don't care," she answered truthfully, still facing the window.

"That must be some test you're studying for," he began uncertainly. "You were in here all weekend. What subject is it in?"

Lila inspected her chipped, unpolished fingernails. They looked like somebody had been biting them. She realized with a start that it had been her. *But I never bite my fingernails*, she thought.

"Lila?" her father asked.

"What?"

"I asked what subject your test is in."

"History," she said to the window. "We're studying the Civil War."

She heard bedsprings creak and knew that her father was sitting on the corner of her unmade canopy bed, staring at her back.

"Lila," he said kindly. "How about taking a break? You know, I haven't been to La Maison Blanche in weeks. I know how much you like their French onion soup—"

"No, thanks, Dad. I'm not hungry."

She heard her father stand up. A moment later, he rested his hand on her shoulder.

"Honey, I'm worried about you," he said. "You've hardly said a word to anyone in the last week. And Lucinda says you haven't been eating."

That was just like her father, Lila thought. The only way he kept up with his own daughter's life was through the servants. She shrugged off his hand and whirled to face him. "I'm fine!" she insisted. "Just leave me alone!"

Her father's eyes opened wide, and Lila remembered that he hadn't seen her up close in several days. He wordlessly took in the dark circles under her eyes, her sunken cheeks and limp, greasy hair. "Lila," he said quietly after a moment. "Mr. Cooper called this evening and said you stayed out of school again. You told me you were going back today."

Lila turned to the window again. "I couldn't go today. I just couldn't. . . ." Her voice trailed off into a whisper.

Lila looked down at the swimming pool. The sky was completely dark now, and a bright spotlight on the side of the house illuminated the swimming pool below so that it looked like a brilliant block of turquoise. She imagined jumping from her window and floating gracefully through the darkness, to be enveloped, alone, in the pool's blue-green coolness.

Lila could feel her father's gaze on her back. "I guess you're mad at me," she said.

"Why would I be mad at you?" he asked, sounding surprised. "Don't worry, honey. I won't force you to go back to school if you're not ready. But we've got to talk about this."

All her life, Lila had wanted her father to pay more attention to her. Now his sympathy was worse than indifference. What did he expect her to say to him?

She shook her head hopelessly. "You wouldn't understand, Dad."

"How do you know that if you don't try?" her father asked.

Lila just shook her head. She couldn't tell him about what had happened with John Pfeifer that terrible night at Miller's Point, before she had managed to break away and get out of the car. She couldn't tell him about her mixed-up feelings for Nathan after he began counseling her about the attempted date rape.

She couldn't tell her father how embarrassed she had felt at school in the days after the prom, with everyone staring at her, thinking she was lying about what Nathan had done.

And she couldn't tell her father, who had never been afraid of anything, that school scared her. People scared her. When she was around all those people at school, she felt as if she were enveloped in a hot wave of terror that she couldn't control.

The girls at school were bad enough. They were always comparing outfits to see who looked the sexiest, whose skirt was the shortest, or who was the thinnest and had the best legs. But the boys were the worst. They were always watching her. Lately when she saw a boy looking at her, Lila wanted to run and hide.

She couldn't tell her father any of it. There was too much he didn't know and too much he could never understand.

"Nobody's blaming you for anything, Lila," her father was saying softly. "I'm worried about you, and I don't know what to do. Please tell me what's wrong."

"I don't know," Lila whispered, her eyes filling with tears. "I don't *know* what's wrong."

George Fowler put his hands on his daughter's slim shoulders and gently turned her to face him. "Tell me about it," he said.

"Daddy, I just can't talk to you about this."

"But why?" he asked gently. "I love you, Lila. You can talk to me about anything."

Lila shook her head again. "I just can't," she said.

Mr. Fowler looked at her for a minute longer. Then he sighed and left the room.

Lila silently watched him go, before turning back to the window. She closed her eyes and rested her hot forehead against the cool glass.

"I *could* talk to my mother," she said. "If I had one."

"This is the most fabulous raspberry mousse I've ever tasted!" Pamela raved, dipping her spoon into it again. It was Tuesday night, and Bruce still couldn't believe that he was on a date with Pamela Robertson.

He laughed, gesturing toward his own dish. "I just can't believe we ordered the same thing *again*—not after the grilled salmon."

Pamela smiled flirtatiously. "Great minds think alike," she said.

Bruce noticed the sensuous way Pamela's full lips parted around the silver spoon as she took another taste of her dessert. When the candlelight reflected for a moment in her unusual blue eyes, something in them—he didn't know what—suddenly reminded Bruce of Regina Morrow. Then she blinked and smiled again, and he decided he'd been wrong. Pamela was nothing like Regina.

Thinking of Regina always made Bruce feel sad and a little guilty. He had liked Regina, but he couldn't stand being tied down. If Bruce hadn't started dating Amy Sutton, Regina might never have gotten involved with the kids who gave her the drugs that had killed her.

But Regina was nothing like Pamela, he told himself. This relationship just felt different. From the moment he had heard Pamela's melodic voice on the darkened football field the night of the dance, Bruce had known that he and Pamela were fated to be together. And he couldn't imagine wanting to be with anyone else again, ever.

"So, we like all the same foods," Pamela said, "including dessert! And we both adore tennis, early-morning picnics on the beach, long-stemmed red roses, and fast cars. What's next, Bruce?"

"Movies," Bruce said. "What's your favorite old classic?"

"*Philadelphia Story,*" Pamela answered without hesitation.

"Awesome!" said Bruce. He shook his head. "You know, I'm not even surprised anymore."

"Don't tell me that's your old favorite too!"

"It really is," said Bruce. He reached out to put his hand over hers, and his voice became serious. "I knew you were a woman of taste."

Pamela looked deep into his eyes, and

Bruce realized that he had never wanted to kiss a girl as much as he wanted to kiss her. But this wasn't the place for that. Besides, for once, Bruce didn't want to rush things. He felt certain that he and Pamela would have plenty of time together in the future.

"Tell me all about yourself," he said intently. "I want to know everything."

She looked away from him and shook her head. "There's nothing much to tell," she said quickly. "I'm just your typical high-school senior."

"Oh, no," Bruce objected. "*Nothing* about you is typical, Pamela."

Pamela seemed uncomfortable. "Um—did I tell you how much I like your choice of restaurants?" she asked, changing the subject away from herself.

Bruce grinned. "At least seven times."

"Well, it deserves an eighth. I've never seen such a romantic place—this big, beautiful old house with the honeysuckle all around. Even the name is romantic—Castillo San Angelo. It just *rolls* off my tongue." She looked at him slyly. "I bet you take all your girlfriends here," she teased.

Bruce shrugged his shoulders. "Other girlfriends?" he asked. "It's funny, but from the minute I saw you—no, from the minute I *heard* you—no other girl mattered."

"From the minute you *heard* me? What do you mean?"

"What?" Bruce asked in mock despair. "You've already forgotten our first date? But it was so romantic. We were outside, behind the school, when I first heard your voice. The night was dark, there was excitement in the air, and we were all alone—just you, me, and a 250-pound linebacker with my name on his baseball bat!"

"And two dozen brawling maniacs," said Pamela, smiling. "I think I like *this* first date much better."

"Me too," Bruce agreed, admiring the way her silky hair fell around her tanned shoulders. "Me too."

"Then that's something else we have in common," said Pamela.

Two hours later, Bruce stood with Pamela on her front doorstep. The ride back had been as wonderful as the meal. Bruce had never found anyone so easy to talk to, and Pamela seemed just as enchanted with him as he was with her.

"I guess this is good night," he said, placing a hand on her smooth shoulder.

Pamela gently stroked his arm. "You said the same thing twenty minutes ago, Bruce."

"And *you* said it twenty minutes before that."

She smiled. "I guess I just don't want this night to end. I've had a fantastic time, Bruce."

"Me too."

"Look at the stars. I've never seen so many!"

"They're beautiful," he said.

"You're not even looking at the stars!"

"Yes I am," he said, gazing into her eyes. Then he put his arms around her slender shoulders and kissed her.

Pamela's lips were warm and soft. She pressed her hands against his back as they kissed, and he felt a delicious tingling where she touched him. Something electric passed between them, and Bruce had the sensation of flying among the stars. No kiss had ever rocked him this way.

When he opened his eyes and looked at her a minute later, he could see in her face that she had felt something special too.

"Bruce," she murmured. "I think I'd better

go inside now—before we fall in love."

"Pamela, I think it's too late."

"I think so too," she replied slowly, smiling up at him. She hugged him once more, then opened the door and stepped inside.

Bruce exhaled as he watched the door shut behind her. Clearly, this was going to be a very special relationship. He was in a daze as he walked back to the curb, climbed into the Porsche, and headed toward Sweet Valley.

How can everything be so perfect? he wondered. *What an evening! What a girl!*

As he turned onto his own street and drove up the winding hill past Sweet Valley's biggest mansions, he realized that he had fallen in love with a girl who was still something of a mystery.

The next time, I'll keep my big mouth shut so she can get a word in edgewise, he decided. *I've told her all about me. The next time, I'll get Pamela to tell me about herself.*

The next time, he thought, smiling broadly. They hadn't even had to say it aloud; of course there would be a next time—and soon. Hundreds of next times, if Bruce had anything to say about it. Already he couldn't wait to see her again.

*　　*　　*

The man at the Port Authority bus-station ticket counter was picking his teeth and looking down at a paper. He didn't even notice her.

Margo wanted to tell him that he was crude and obnoxious, but she bit her tongue. She had to watch what she said; she wasn't dressed as a boy anymore, and she didn't want to be identified.

It was Tuesday night. Margo had waited in a motel room outside New York City for three days—long enough to make sure that no one was looking for her. The fire had been on the news—which gave Margo a tremendous feeling of power. The reports had been that one body had been recovered before the entire house collapsed. Fire investigators were sifting through the rubble, searching for the remains of the Logans' sixteen-year-old foster daughter. On the off chance that somebody, someday, might have some reason to be suspicious, Margo didn't want this slob behind the counter, or anyone else, to be able to recognize her. So, as much as she longed to tell him what she really thought of him, she would not. She wouldn't say anything that might call at-

131

tention to herself and make him remember her.

"Excuse me," she said politely. "I'd like to buy a ticket."

"Yep," he said, eyeing her up and down. "Where you heading?"

None of your business! "Cleveland."

"Round trip?"

No way! "One way."

She had already checked the departure time and the gate number, so after buying her ticket, she took an escalator to the level where the Cleveland bus would depart from.

She sat down on a plastic seat near the departing gate until she heard a voice crackle over the loudspeaker announcing the departure of the bus for Cleveland.

Cleveland, repeated the raspy voice inside her head.

Something was drawing Margo west. She wasn't sure what it was—a new life, a new home, or a new identity. But it was calling to her, and she knew that she would know it when she arrived wherever she was going.

A sharp pain darted through her head, and Margo put her hand to her temple. The familiar pounding was back. She closed her eyes;

bright red splotches pulsed against the inside of her eyelids.

Red like pain, whispered the voice. *Red like fire. Red like blood.*

Margo opened her eyes, stood up, and walked toward the gate. Something she had always wanted waited for her, somewhere west of here. But what was it that she'd always wanted?

Patience, the voice said. The pain began to subside. *Patience.*

Margo would be patient. She would get to Ohio and find a way to make some more money. She didn't know how long she would stay there. But after she had enough money for the next stage of her journey, she would move on. She would move further west. And she would keep moving west until she found what she was looking for.

Chapter 8

Olivia stopped her father's white Oldsmobile in front of a long, circular driveway that led to a huge, elegant house. She peered at the house number on the open wrought-iron gate. Then she fumbled through the little black purse her mother had lent her, searching for the address of the Coastal California Fine Arts Foundation.

"Leave it to me to get lost on the way to my first big-time art event," she muttered, shaking her head.

She found the scribbled address on a scrap of sketchbook paper and compared it to the number on the gate in front of the white-pillared mansion: 16 Bridgewater Estates Avenue. This was it, Olivia thought. Although it certainly didn't look like an arts foundation. It looked more like the movie set for *Gone with the Wind*. Then she laughed at herself and shook her head. She certainly wasn't an expert on what an arts foundation should look like.

She parked by the curb and stepped out of the car. Then she felt a rush of air and quickly pressed her body against the side of the Oldsmobile as a car sped by.

"Wow, I didn't even see that one coming!" she said aloud.

Then Olivia looked down at her new clothes in a panic. How could she be so clumsy? How could she lean against the side of a car when she had on a brand-new outfit, on an important night like this?

Olivia took a deep breath to calm her nerves. It was all right; her father had just washed the car, and her outfit was still clean. She straightened her skirt and stepped around the Oldsmobile to the curb.

Olivia had finally devised a good, semiprofessional compromise between her usual artsy attire—tie-dyed shirts, leggings, peasant skirts, and funky jewelry—and her parents' business-suit conservativeness. She was wearing a blazer, but it was loose and long, and was printed with a riot of wild colors and abstract shapes. She wore it over a deep purple shell top, a straight black skirt, and purple tights.

Even her mother—the manager of what Olivia liked to think of as the Hopelessly Dull Women's Sportswear Department at Simpson's Department Store—had been impressed.

"You look exactly as a rising young painter should for this kind of event—artistic, but pulled together," had been Mrs. Davidson's appraisal before Olivia had left the house that evening.

Olivia had smiled and hugged her. As buttoned down as her parents were, they had always supported her painting, her poetry, and her "outlandish" tendencies. Olivia knew that they were proud of her recent success and that they were as excited as she was about the invitation to speak in front of some of the leaders of the local artistic community.

Excited? she asked herself. *Is that what I am? I thought this was* terror!"

Suddenly Olivia looked around her, confused. Hers was the only car parked anywhere near 16 Bridgewater Estates Avenue. Where were the cars that the art patrons must have driven to get there? she wondered.

She checked the scribbled note she was still clutching. It was the right evening and the right time. The reception was scheduled for six, and her speech was at seven. She looked at her watch—six fifteen. Maybe no one had shown up.

That was silly. They wouldn't have asked her to come if there wasn't going to be anyone there. They probably had some other parking area that she didn't know about. She shoved the scrap of paper back into her mother's purse, wiped her sweaty hands on a tissue, and walked up the long driveway.

She glanced up at the sky. It had become overcast and looked as if it would start to rain any minute. "Just what I need," she muttered. Why hadn't she brought an umbrella?

Then she laughed and shook her head. She couldn't remember a single rainy day in her life when she *had* remembered an umbrella. Why should today be any different? Besides, umbrellas were for insurance people and accountants—and bankers like her father. Artists didn't carry umbrellas.

She walked up the steps of the mansion's wide front porch and stood in front of the door. It was huge, with a brass pineapple for a door knocker.

Olivia knocked on the door and waited a few minutes. She got no reply.

She felt awkward and nervous. Why was no one answering the door? She stood there a few moments longer. Finally she made a decision: It was a foundation, not a private house. It was probably all right for her to just go in.

Olivia took a deep breath and pushed the door open.

The huge entrance hall was dominated by the biggest and most beautiful stairway Olivia had ever seen. White marble steps stretched upward in a graceful arc, with a path of velvety green carpeting leading up the center of them. Intricately carved posts and banisters framed the stairwell, and a crystal chandelier as big as Olivia's bedroom hung overhead.

Olivia whistled involuntarily, then froze when a boy came into view, walking toward her down the broad staircase. It was the shy, handsome, sandy-haired guy from her class at the art school—the one who was always looking at her from across the room

The boy blushed, and for a moment Olivia thought he was surprised to see her there. Then he cleared his throat nervously.

"You've come," he said.

The nearer Jessica got to the dirt-bike track, the slower she drove. This was the night of the big race, the Pacific Classic that Sam had been practicing for the week he died. There would be a memorial service before the race; Sam's racing friends had given Jessica a special invitation.

The track complex was up ahead. The evening was still light, despite the overcast sky. But intense white lights had already been switched on to illuminate the bike track. Jessica blinked in the glare. It must be the lights that were making her eyes water, she decided.

She was still three blocks away from the entrance, but she could already tell that the parking lot was full. Cars were spilling out onto the street. Jessica had enough experience with dirt-bike racing to know that this turnout was unusual. Of course, this was an important race, but she knew that a lot of these people were coming because of Sam.

Jessica imagined herself in the bleachers, listening to people talking about how generous and sweet and friendly Sam had been.

I can't do it, she thought. She just couldn't attend Sam's memorial service. She was too grief stricken to listen to other people talk about him—people who didn't know him as well as she had and who couldn't understand what she was feeling. And she was too angry at the person she knew was to blame for his death.

Jessica pressed the accelerator of the rental car and sped past the racetrack. She turned up a beautiful old residential street, still speeding, and swerved to keep from hitting a big, classy-looking white car.

She drove without thinking, with no idea of where she was heading. Ten minutes later she stopped the car and looked around to get her bearings. Suddenly she felt numb. Without planning it, she found that she was at the cemetery in Bridgewater, the place where Sam was buried.

The cemetery gates were still open, and quickly, before she could change her mind, Jessica drove in and stopped at the small office building. The man inside gave her directions to Sam's grave. She drove to the section he had indicated. Then she parked, took a deep breath to calm her nerves, and got out of the car. Slowly she walked up a slight hill to the gravesite.

There was no headstone yet, but Sam's grave was easy to spot. There was a rectangular carpet of new, bright-green grass set amid graying tombstones. Several withering potted plants were sitting near the site.

For several minutes Jessica stood, looking down at the grave. Then in a soft voice, she began to speak to the boy she had loved.

"It's not fair," she said, reaching down to finger the wilted petals of a potted carnation. "You were too young, Sam. People our age aren't supposed to die."

A tear ran down her cheek and Jessica wiped it away angrily. "It's Liz's fault!" she said. "Liz took you away from me!"

She clenched her fists and tried to hold on to the anger. Jessica knew that her anger was the only thing that had allowed her to get through the weeks since Sam's death. She was afraid of letting go of it. She was afraid of what might lie beneath it.

Jessica felt another drop of water on her

face and realized that it had started to drizzle.

She suddenly remembered the rain on her face one evening a few months earlier, as she and Sam had walked along the beach. She had shivered in her bikini top and shorts; Sam draped his sweater around her shoulders and hugged her close for warmth. But it was the warmth in his gray eyes that had stopped her shivering.

She remembered Sam, dressed as Batman, bringing her flowers when he was afraid she would leave him for Brandon Hunter, the stuck-up soap-opera star. And she thought of how Sam had come to her rescue when the Good Friends cult had tried to take her away from Sweet Valley.

Then Jessica thought of all the times she had made up excuses for not seeing him because she didn't want to stand around at a dirt-bike race, getting her clothes muddy. She would give anything to get muddy now, if it meant that she would be able to see Sam again.

"You always came through for me, Sam," she said to the silent grave. "And look what I did to you!"

Sam was dead, and *she* was responsible for

the accident that had killed him.

"I can blame it on Elizabeth, but I know it's my fault," she said, sobbing. "*I* was the one who wanted to be Prom Queen so badly that I sabotaged my own sister! *I* was the one who put alcohol in her drink. I should have tried harder to keep her from driving that night!"

The light drizzle mixed with the tears that ran down her face. "I don't know what to do, Sam!" she said between sobs. "How could I do something so horrible and let Liz think it's her fault? But I can't tell her it isn't. I can't tell anybody! I could never face her again!"

She had nobody to talk to, nobody she dared to tell the truth to. Elizabeth would hate her if she knew what Jessica had done. And Sam was gone forever. Jessica felt more alone than she had ever felt in her life.

The truth of Sam's death suddenly hit Jessica with a terrible finality. Sam would never again drape his sweater around her shoulders and hug her close. He would never again make her laugh with one of his crazy ideas. He would never again rescue her when she was in trouble.

Jessica crumpled to the ground next to

Sam's grave and cried burning tears into the cool, damp grass. The fine drizzle slowly soaked through the thin cotton straps of her gray tank top and plastered her long hair to her head.

"Oh, Sam," she cried, "I miss you so much!"

The sky grew darker overhead, and the drizzle turned into a torrential downpour that masked the sound of Jessica's wrenching sobs.

"So, another date with Pamela?" asked Roger Barrett Patman, sauntering through the doorway of his cousin's room that evening.

"That's right!" said Bruce, grinning into the full-length mirror as he tied a perfect windsor knot in his brand-new Italian silk tie. "This is it, Roger. This girl is something special."

Roger sat on the edge of Bruce's bed and watched him for a moment. "You know, Bruce," he began hesitantly, "you really shouldn't rush into a relationship like this. Take it slowly. Pamela's not going any-where—"

"You're right!" said Bruce, smoothing his dark hair. "Not if I have anything to say about it."

Normally his cousin's interference would have annoyed him, but Bruce was feeling magnanimous lately. He was about to go out on his second date with California's sweetest and most beautiful girl—not to mention an amazing kisser. And she was as crazy about him as he was about her.

Roger was probably a little envious, Bruce decided. He had never had Bruce's way with girls. But then again, not many guys did.

"Stick with me, cousin!" Bruce said, winking at Roger's reflection in the mirror. "I'll teach you everything there is to know about women."

He searched around the room until he found his newly polished black dress shoes, then sat on the bed next to Roger to put them on.

"This is only your second date with her," Roger reminded him. "There may be some things you don't know about her."

For an instant, Bruce thought that Roger had a point. He remembered driving home after his date with Pamela Tuesday night and realizing that he hadn't learned much about her at all.

Well, he decided, *that's what second dates are for.*

"That's the thing about women," he said, playfully slapping Roger on the back. "You never want to know *too* much about them too soon. It spoils the *mystery*!"

His tone suddenly became serious. "But when it comes to the important things, Roger, I know everything I need to know about this girl."

Roger shrugged and stood up. "OK. You're your own man, Bruce. I guess you know what you're doing." He walked to the door, opened it, then turned to face Bruce. "But take it slow," he said again. "Remember, appearances can be deceiving."

Bruce stared at the heavy paneled door as it swung shut behind his cousin.

Now what was all that about? he wondered. *Does Roger know something I don't know?*

His shiny black shoe slipped from his hand and landed loudly on the parquet floor, and Bruce started at the noise.

"Nah," he said, shaking his head. *Roger has a whole lot to learn about women.*

Bruce shrugged his shoulders, picked up the fallen shoe, and began to whistle cheerfully as he finished preparing for his second date with the girl of his dreams.

Chapter 9

"You've come," said the handsome sandy-haired guy for the second time as he descended the sweeping staircase. As he walked, he smiled down at her shyly.

Olivia shifted nervously from foot to foot. "I think I may have gotten something mixed up," she said. She began fumbling through her mother's purse, looking for the scribbled directions.

"No, you haven't gotten anything mixed up," he said a little awkwardly.

"I was looking for the Coastal California Fine Arts Foundation," Olivia told him. "Am I in the right place?"

"Well, you're in the right place—" the boy began.

"Are you here to give a speech too?"

"Well, not exactly," said the boy, blushing again. He reached the bottom of the stairs and faced Olivia.

Olivia noticed once again that he was awfully cute. He was shorter than he had seemed in class, she thought. He was really only a few inches taller than she was; his broad shoulders had made him seem bigger. *This is no time to be looking at his shoulders,* Olivia told herself sternly. She stared him straight in the eyes.

"Then what exactly is going on?" she demanded.

"I guess I'd better explain," he said. "You see, uh, this is my home. . . ."

Olivia stared at him. "*Your home?* I don't understand. Do you mean you tricked me?" she asked incredulously. "And that there is no Coastal California Fine Arts Foundation?"

The boy looked at his hands for a moment before meeting her gaze. He had the largest, clearest gray eyes Olivia had ever seen.

"Not exactly," he said finally. "I mean, yes, I *did* trick you. And no, there's not exactly a fine arts foundation."

Olivia had been ready to storm out of the house, but something about his tone of voice stopped her. He sounded so sincere. And despite her anger, she was curious about what was going on.

"Not exactly?" she asked. "But that's ridiculous! No one would make up a story like that just to get me to come over to his house!"

"I'm really sorry," he said. "The last thing I wanted to do was upset you." His huge, light-gray eyes pleaded with her as he gestured toward a doorway off to one side of the staircase. "Come into the sunroom and sit down, and I'll explain everything to you," he said.

Olivia shrugged. "Well, you've already wasted my time and made a fool of me. Why shouldn't I stick around and see how else you plan to humiliate me?"

"By the way," he added with a sheepish grin that made Olivia want to smile in spite of her anger. "I'm Harry—Harry Minton."

"I still don't get it, Harry," Olivia said fifteen minutes later. "You decide that you want to buy my painting, so you make up this elaborate story about a speaking engagement just to get me to come *here*." She gestured around the wicker-filled sunroom where they were sitting. "But you still haven't told me *why.*"

Harry laughed, and Olivia noticed again what a great smile he had.

"Well, why not?" he said.

"*Why not?* Because you see me every single week in art class, that's why not. Why didn't you just ask me to drop by if you wanted to talk?"

Harry ran a hand through his thick hair. "You always seem so *focused* in class," he said. "You're so intent on what you're doing that I'm afraid to interrupt. I mean, I'd never forgive myself if I distracted you and screwed up one of your paintings. It would be like being personally responsible for the deterioration of the Sistine Chapel ceiling."

"I wouldn't put my paintings on quite *that* high a level," said Olivia.

"Not yet, maybe," Harry answered seriously. "But they'll be considered masterpieces someday. You know, Olivia, I see the work people are doing in all my classes, and yours stands out. It's different, really inspired. I love art, and

I'm serious about my work, but you've got the potential to be a much, much better painter than I'll ever be."

Olivia gestured at him with one of the peach-and-white pillows that adorned the wicker love seat she was sitting on. "Don't try to flatter me," she said. "I'm still mad at you for getting me here under false pretenses."

"I'm not trying to flatter you, honest!" Harry said. "I truly believe that you have a lot of talent, Olivia. You know, I practically fell off my seat when I heard you were still in high school. I sure wasn't painting like that when I was in high school!"

"You make it sound like that was decades ago," Olivia said, curious to know just how old Harry was.

"Centuries," said Harry. "How do you think I knew about the Sistine Chapel?"

"Were *you* the one who painted that?" Olivia asked. "And all these years I thought it was Michelangelo."

"Most people think so," Harry confided. "That's only because he had a better press agent than I did."

Olivia smiled. "I see," she said. She finished her iced tea and set the glass down on a small, marble-topped table. "So what do you do with yourself, Harry—besides painting cherubs on ceilings and inventing fictional art foundations?"

"Nothing too exciting, until this evening," Harry said. He blushed and looked down at his hands. "I graduated from high school last year. My parents wanted me to go away to college somewhere with ivy smeared all over the walls. I think they were hoping I'd get steeped in all that tradition and would suddenly realize I had a lawyer inside of me struggling to get out!"

"Sounds crowded."

Harry grinned at her gratefully and went on. "Well, I don't have to tell *you* what it's like to want to be in the art world," he said. "And the art school here is as good as anywhere else. So I told my parents I was staying, and they were pretty good about it."

"Are you taking painting classes full-time?" Olivia asked enviously.

"Watercolor, drawing, design, and art history," Harry answered. "But I'm majoring in creative ways to get to know intriguing young artists!"

"I bet you say that to *all* the young artists you watch from afar," said Olivia.

Harry shook his head. "Nope. I'm just not that easily intrigued. And I really do want to buy your painting—even if you won't go out to dinner with me tomorrow night. But I hope you will."

"That's about the weirdest invitation I can remember getting," she said, throwing a pillow at him. "Has anyone ever told you that you're absolutely insane?"

"In this neighborhood, we say *eccentric*," Harry said and smiled broadly. Olivia couldn't help smiling back.

"Whatever you call it," she said, "I think I like it."

George Fowler slipped into his study and stopped for a moment to listen. The big house was silent. Lila was asleep upstairs—at least, he hoped his daughter was asleep. She hadn't seemed to have slept more than a few hours total in the last few weeks.

He locked the door behind him, walked to his gleaming mahogany desk, and sat down slowly, thinking of his only child. He had tried to speak with Lila again earlier that evening. Again he'd been shocked at the way she looked.

He had always been proud of his little girl. Of course, he conceded, Lila was a bit on the vain side. She would spend hours working on the perfect suntan, the perfect hairstyle, the perfect outfit. But Lila had reason to be vain; after all, he thought proudly, she was the prettiest, most popular girl in town.

But now Lila was a different person. All week she had been sitting motionless in the same window seat, wearing the same gray sweat suit. As far as George knew, his daughter hadn't spoken with any of her friends since that one phone call Monday night.

Lila's hair was unkempt, and her usually tanned face was ashen, except for the circles under her eyes, which became more pronounced every day. She had lost weight, too. She had always been slender, but now she looked as if she were withering away.

Her eyes were the worst, her father thought. Lila's big brown eyes used to look confident and alive. Now all he could see in them was fear and confusion. And she wouldn't tell him what she was afraid of or what he could do to help her.

Why did she keep pushing him away? Why did she always assume that he would be angry with her, or uncaring, or unbelieving? If he had seemed unresponsive, he knew it was because he was as confused as Lila was. He didn't know how to approach her or what to say. He didn't know how to help her.

Of course, he'd been upset when he found out that his daughter had wrongly accused the guidance counselor of attacking her. But he wasn't angry with Lila, and he was sure that she knew that.

He still didn't understand why she had done it, but it wasn't as if she had made up the story. He had talked with Mr. Cooper and with Nathan Pritchard, and both men felt that Lila had really believed herself to be in danger. But why? What would make a confident, well-adjusted teenager suddenly become so fearful?

George admitted that he didn't know his daughter as well as he could. Of course, Lila knew how much he loved her. But his business kept him traveling so much; he was seldom home for more than a few days in a row. He had always given her anything she wanted, though—designer clothes, jewelry, the latest electronic equipment. And she had always seemed happy with what he gave her.

Since the meeting in Mr. Cooper's office, he had tried over and over again to speak with her. She kept telling him he wouldn't understand. Of course he would understand. She was his daughter and he loved her more than anything.

He had suggested that she go to a new counselor, and she had burst into tears. Finally he had decided that if he gave her some time, she would work out was bothering her and then go back to being a bright, active, normal teenager.

But now it was time to face facts: Lila couldn't pull herself out of this alone. She wouldn't go to a new counselor, and she couldn't go back to Nathan Pritchard. Yet. She needed help, and he, her own father, wasn't able to give it to her. He just couldn't break down the wall she had built between them. Now his daughter was in serious trouble. If he couldn't help her himself and if she wouldn't see a counselor, he would have to call someone who *could* help her.

He pulled his address file closer and began thumbing through it.

It was difficult for George Fowler to admit that he couldn't handle this situation. Ever since the divorce—no, before that—ever since he had sent Lila's mother away, he thought he'd done pretty well as a single parent. But he obviously wasn't qualified to handle the current situation.

He pulled out an address card and read it. He wasn't sure how Lila would react to this. But he couldn't put off the decision anymore. For Lila's sake, he had to bring in somebody who would have a chance of reaching her.

George took a deep breath. Then he picked up the phone and asked for the long-distance operator.

"Hello," he said. "I have to call Paris. I need to place a person-to-person call to a Ms. Grace Fowler."

He gave the operator the number of Lila's mother, at her boyfriend's estate, and hoped he was doing the right thing.

"I have to admit, your letters of reference look impressive, Michelle," said Sheila Rossi the next morning, handing the papers back to the girl.

Margo smiled demurely. *They'd better look impressive,* she thought. *I spent two hours at the typewriter store yesterday, making them up.* "Thank you," she said.

"And how long did you say you baby-sat for the Foster family before moving here to Cleveland?"

"Just over a year," Margo said. "Nina was the sweetest little girl," she said, smiling with just the right touch of wistfulness. "She had the biggest brown eyes you've ever seen, and baby-fine hair like spun gold. I loved to play games with her, to cook her dinner, and to read her fairy tales." She smiled. "Hansel and Gretel was Nina's favorite. She always loved the part about the witch wanting to cook the children for dinner."

Ms. Rossi chuckled. "Yes, children do love to be scared, don't they?" the tall, elegantly dressed woman said. "My little boy, Georgie, is eight. He's really quite well-behaved most of the time, but he *does* get stubborn every now and then, like all children. It sounds as if you have the experience to handle him, though."

"Oh, yes, ma'am," Margo said sweetly. "I know just how to handle children. I've always loved kids. I've been baby-sitting since I was ten years old—that makes eight years!"

"So you're eighteen years old," said Ms.

Rossi. "You graduated from high school last semester, I take it?"

Margo nodded.

"Splendid," said Ms. Rossi. "I hate trusting my babies to someone who's still a child herself. You know," she continued, "my older son, Josh, is just your age. There's his picture—"

She pointed to an expensively framed photograph of the two boys, which was on the table next to Margo. Josh was tall and dark, with what Margo liked to think of as a "bad boy" gleam in his eyes.

Forget the eight-year-old brat, Margo thought. *I wouldn't mind doing a little babysitting with big-brother Josh.*

"What a nice-looking family!" Margo said sweetly. "Little Georgie is just as cute as can be—with all that curly red hair! I can't wait to meet him. And I can see where Josh got his good looks!"

Ms. Rossi beamed. "I do wish you could meet them both today," she said. "Josh is out with Georgie right now. He took him to buy sneakers for school. Actually, I had asked *him* to look after Georgie on a regular basis, a few days a week, but he says he's much too busy."

She smiled proudly. "You know how active teenage boys are!"

What I know about teenage boys would curl your hair, lady, Margo bragged silently.

"Now, Michelle," said Ms. Rossi, "you said you've only been in Cleveland a short time. What made you leave New York?"

Margo turned her head away and allowed a single tear to slip out from beneath her closed eyelids. *Too bad they don't give Academy Awards for job interviews,* she thought. She swallowed hard and then looked straight at Ms. Rossi.

"My mother died two months ago," Margo said quietly, brushing the tear away with her hand. "I had nowhere else to go, so I moved here to live with my older sister. I've just enrolled in a community college, and I need the extra money to pay for my books and help out my sister."

"You poor dear," said Ms. Rossi. "I am so sorry about your mother."

Cut the garbage, lady, and tell me I've got the job, Margo urged silently.

"But I'm glad that you answered my newspaper ad, Michelle. You wouldn't believe the phone calls I've gotten!"

Ms. Rossi grimaced and shook her head. "As I said in the ad," she continued, "I need somebody who can work every afternoon after school, and several evenings a week. It's a big time commitment, and frankly, I'm picky about who I entrust my son to. It's hard to find somebody responsible who really wants to be around small children."

I like being around them, all right, Margo thought. *Like a boa constrictor.*

"What part of town are you living in, Michelle?" asked Ms. Rossi.

Margo threw up her hands. "I'm afraid I just don't know my way around the city yet, Ms. Rossi," she said with a self-deprecating smile. "But the place where I'm staying isn't nearly as nice as *your* lovely home," she added.

That's an understatement, she thought. Since Wednesday, she had been living in a cramped room at the YWCA. By comparison, this place was a regular Buckingham Palace.

"How nice of you to say so! I'd love to show you around, but I've got a charity luncheon today. I'll give you the full tour on Monday—if you can start Monday. Is that too soon?"

"Monday will be *perfect*!"

"Georgie is going to love you. I know it already," said Ms. Rossi as she ushered Margo toward the door. "You won't regret taking this job, Michelle."

"Oh, I'm sure I won't," Margo said, smiling broadly.

As she turned her back on her new employer, Margo's smile disappeared. *I never regret anything,* she added silently.

Margo hardly noticed the stately homes and well-tended gardens of Shaker Heights, a wealthy suburb of Cleveland, as she walked to the bus stop after the interview. Oh, no. She wouldn't regret taking the job. It was just what she had been looking for.

From the looks of the fine crystal, expensive jewelry, and electronic gadgets she had seen around the house, Margo decided the fringe benefits at the Rossi household wouldn't be bad, either. She was sure she could find a way to spread some of those riches around without jeopardizing her job. Like anything else, it would take nothing more than a little planning and a little patience.

As she walked, Margo's head began to

throb. Then she heard the rasp of that familiar, internal voice. *One step closer,* it said with grim satisfaction, in time to the pounding of her headache. *One step closer.*

Chapter 10

"Could it be?" asked Winston in the school cafeteria Friday. "Is this the rich and powerful Lord Bruce of Patman, deigning to eat lunch with us peasants?"

Bruce laughed. "That's right, peasant," he said, playfully knocking Winston on the head with his lunch tray. "Move over and make some room!"

"You aristocrats are always pushing people around!" Winston complained, sliding his chair a few inches closer to his girlfriend, Maria Santelli. He pointed with his spoon at Maria, Amy, and Jessica. "Shall I hire some of these lovely young peasant girls to feed you peeled grapes?"

"Thanks for the offer, good man," said Bruce, sliding into the seat next to Winston. "But I'm a one-woman kind of guy."

Barry Rork choked on his sandwich, recovered after a minute, and stared at Bruce. "Since when?" he asked incredulously.

Bruce just raised his eyebrows, enjoying his secret.

"OK, Bruce, who is she?" Amy asked.

"So *that's* it, Patman!" Winston said. "You've had that silly grin on your face for a week! And this sickening *niceness* is going to destroy your reputation! I heard you were chasing after some new woman—did you finally catch her? That would explain all this unseemly happiness."

"Either that, or the Dow Jones is up," Maria said dryly.

"Come on, Patman, out with it!" urged Ken Matthews. Ken was the quarterback for the Sweet Valley High Gladiators, and a close friend of Bruce.

Bruce grinned. Let them be mystified a little longer, he thought. He turned to Todd. "So what about you, Wilkins?" he asked. "This isn't exactly *your* usual lunch crowd, either."

"Jessica was by herself, and I dropped by

to say hello," Todd said guardedly. "I can't help it if the rest of you riffraff decided to join us."

Until then, Bruce had barely noticed Jessica, although she sat directly across the table from him, picking listlessly at her salad. He felt sorry for her; he knew she had really loved Sam Woodruff. She seemed like a different person since his death. Bruce used to complain that Jessica was overbearing and a pest, but now he realized that he actually missed her sarcastic remarks.

"How are you holding up, Jessica?" he asked kindly.

Jessica stared up at him in surprise, as if she expected some kind of a joke. Her usually tanned face was pale, and her blue-green eyes were rimmed in red. She shrugged. "I'm all right, Bruce," she said with a weak smile. "Thanks for asking."

Then she got up, picked up her tray, and without another word left the table. Bruce noticed that Todd's brown eyes followed her, full of concern.

Bruce suddenly realized that he hadn't seen Todd and Elizabeth together in weeks, although that wasn't surprising, considering the way Elizabeth had acted at the prom. Todd had always been kind of a wimp, Bruce thought, but it was decent of him to keep an eye on Jessica. With the twins acting like strangers toward each other, it was lucky somebody was looking out for her.

"Come on, Bruce," said Amy, intruding on his thoughts. "Stop changing the subject. What's this dream girl's name?"

Bruce cleared his throat and waited until he had everyone's attention.

"Pamela," he finally announced, beaming. "Pamela Robertson."

Amy's slate-gray eyes widened. "Do you mean Pamela Robertson from Big Mesa?" she asked in astonishment.

"That's right," Bruce confirmed. "Why? Do you know her?"

Amy snorted. "Do I know her? *Everybody* knows Pamela, if you know what I mean!" She winked at Maria, who rolled her eyes.

Bruce noticed a surprised glance pass between Barry and Ken. Even Winston seemed to be stifling a giggle. Only Todd appeared unaffected.

"Hey!" said Bruce. "What gives around here?"

"I hear that Pamela does," said Amy, laughing. "I hear she's a *very* giving person."

There was absolute silence at the table. Every one except Amy looked uncomfortable.

"Uh—maybe it's just a rumor, Bruce," Barry said uncertainly after a minute. He gave Amy a warning glare.

"So, uh, did anyone try that brown stuff they're serving for dessert?" asked Maria. "They say it's peanut-butter pudding, but I have my doubts."

"I'm glad to see they've found a way to recycle the leftover wheat paste from papier-mache projects in art class," Winston quipped.

The conversation moved on, but Bruce was barely listening. He had been looking forward to his date with Pamela the next night. Now he didn't know what to do. He had always prided himself on his choice of women. But this time, he wondered, had he made a terrible mistake?

"The lasagna is terrific," Steven Wakefield said at dinner Saturday night. "Who's the cook?" He looked around the table at the silent faces of his family. "Earth to Wakefields!" he said. "Is anybody there?"

"Sorry, Steven," his mother said with a weak smile. "I guess we're all a little preoccupied. Uh, Elizabeth made the lasagna."

"It's great, Liz," he said.

"Thanks, Steven," Elizabeth murmured.

"In fact, I could use another helping. Would you hand me the dish, Jess?"

Without looking up from her plate, Jessica passed it to him.

"It's such a treat to be home, eating real food—" Steven began. Then he shook his head slightly. "Well, don't everybody jump up and down telling me how glad you are to have me here! You might hurt something."

"It's always good to have you home, Steven," his mother said.

Steven had come home just for one night. He had exams the following week and needed to study. But he had been worried about what was happening to his family and decided to make another attempt to resolve the situation. But he didn't seem to be making much headway, Steven thought.

He tried again a few minutes later. "Remember that TV show you were asking about, Dad?" he asked, reaching for the water pitcher.

172

Ned Wakefield glanced up, a distracted look on his face.

It's as if he's just suddenly noticed that I'm here, Steven thought. *What is wrong with this family?*

"Remember—the program is called *Hunks,*" Steven continued desperately. "It's the show where they set a guy up on blind dates with three different women. Well, I saw an ad in the paper yesterday. The producers are looking for contestants. It might be the chance of a lifetime for some lucky young stud," he joked, flexing his arm muscles. "What do you think, Jessica? Should I go on national television and make the women of America swoon?"

He stopped and waited a moment. "You see, Jess, that's where you're supposed to come in with one of your inane insults. It's called witty banter. You know—I say, 'Should I make the women swoon?' and you say, 'Yeah, with indigestion.'"

Steven's voice trailed off, and he picked at his lasagna. Suddenly he didn't feel like eating. He couldn't believe what was happening to his family. He had been home the weekend before, and the twins had seemed depressed, but at least their parents had still been trying to hold everything together. Now they seemed just as distraught as the girls.

Even Prince Albert, the family's golden retriever, drooped wearily in the corner, watching the family morosely. For once, the dog's tail wasn't wagging.

Steven slowly looked at each of his sisters, then at his parents.

"This is terrible," he said quietly. "This family is a mess. I know how hard everyone's been hit by what's happened. But we can't go on this way."

"Do you have any suggestions?" asked his father in a tired voice.

"We've got to pull together," he said, looking at the twins. There were tears in Jessica's eyes. "We have to be there for one another," Steven said earnestly. "All of us!"

He watched helplessly as Jessica stood up and left the room. A moment later he heard her sobbing as she ran up the stairs.

"We've become so isolated," Steven continued after a minute. "We're each in our own little world." He motioned toward his parents. "You two are throwing yourselves into your jobs. And Jessica and Elizabeth—"

He stared at Elizabeth, and his heart went

out to his sister. There had always been a special bond between them. Now she looked up at him, her face streaked with tears.

"Liz," he said gently, "I've never seen you so depressed. Let us help you."

"Steven, I can't—" she began. Then she shook her head, jumped up, and raced from the room.

Prince Albert pulled himself to his paws and padded out after her.

After a minute Mrs. Wakefield spoke. "You're right, of course," she said. "We just can't seem to reach either of the girls, Steven." She shook her head sorrowfully and looked at her hands. "I don't know what else to try."

"Dad?"

Ned Wakefield absentmindedly twisted the band of his wristwatch. Steven had never thought of his father as old, but he suddenly seemed to have aged twenty years. When Ned looked at his son, Steven saw tears in his eyes.

"We've just run out of things to say," his father admitted.

Steven stared at both of his parents, speechless. He remembered a period earlier that year, when Mr. and Mrs. Wakefield had gotten a trial separation. That had been a difficult time for the family, but this was far worse. And there didn't seem to be anything anyone could do to change the situation.

"I just can't help wondering," Steven said, "if we'll ever be a family again."

"Lila" came her father's voice from the staircase. "I need to speak with you, honey. Would you please come down to my study? It will only take a few minutes."

Lila sighed. What did *he* want? she wondered, staring out the window at the pool in the twilight.

It was Saturday evening, and Lila had stayed out of school the entire week—as well as half of the week before. Maybe her father had spoken with Mr. Cooper again, she thought. Her father had probably figured out that she hadn't even looked at the assignments the principal had sent home for her. Maybe he was going to lecture her about her schoolwork.

She shook her head. *No,* she thought listlessly. *He doesn't sound mad.* In fact, he'd been surprisingly nice about the whole thing. Too nice, in fact. Not long ago, Lila would have been thrilled to see her father being so concerned about her. Back then he hardly seemed to notice her at all. He had always been too busy. Now she just wished he would leave her alone.

He was going to try and talk to her again, she thought, just as he had been trying to do all week. It was becoming a familiar routine. Her father would try to cheer her up by offering to take her on a trip or out to dinner. He would ask her what was wrong and what he could do to help. She supposed it was nice to know that he cared, after all these years. But now she realized that it wasn't enough. *He* wasn't enough.

Her father didn't know what had happened—or almost happened—in the front seat of John Pfeiffer's car last month. And Lila couldn't tell him. And she couldn't tell him about Nathan. He wouldn't understand. He couldn't.

She fought against the feeling of panic that seemed to wash over her so often these days.

I can't tell him why I can't go to school, she thought. *And I can't tell him what I'm afraid of now. I can't tell him what's wrong with me, because I don't know what's wrong with me.*

"Lila?" her father called again. "Did you hear me? Are you all right?"

"I'm coming," she said. The wave of panic passed. Now she just felt numb again. She rose from the window seat and glanced out once more at the shimmering, jewellike pool. Then she pulled down her baggy sweatshirt and headed downstairs.

Outside the door of her father's study, Lila paused and took a deep breath.

"Hi, honey," said her father, opening it. *He must have been standing just inside the door waiting,* she realized. He motioned toward a leather-covered easy chair. "Sit down, please."

"I'll stand," she said quietly.

George Fowler looked surprised. Then he shrugged and also remained standing, shifting nervously from foot to foot. He opened his mouth as if to speak, then closed it.

"How are you feeling?" he asked finally.

"Fine," she murmured, not meeting his gaze.

"Lila, I don't know how you're going to feel about this," he began. "I hope you're not angry with me. But, honey, I'm concerned about you, and it's obvious that I can't help you through this myself."

178

I have no idea what he's talking about, she realized in a detached way. Her father's fingers fluttered nervously at his sides, and Lila was vaguely aware of the chimes of the huge grandfather clock in the mansion's entryway. She couldn't remember ever seeing her father look so nervous.

"Lila, this week I called somebody who might be more able to talk to you about what's bothering you. Don't be mad, honey, but I got word tonight that she's coming."

"Who is it?" she asked, although she didn't really care. It was hard enough just to listen, the way her mind kept wandering.

"Your mother," he answered slowly. "I called your mother, and she'll be here next week—"

Before he could go on, Lila threw herself into his arms, tears streaming down her face. How could he have known that this was exactly what she had hoped for?

"My mother?" she cried, burying her face in his shoulder. "My mother's coming *here*? Oh, thank you, Daddy! Thank you!"

He held her for a long time, and she could tell from the trembling of his arms that he was crying too.

Chapter 11

Bruce lay in bed Saturday night, going over the evening's events in his mind.

His date with Pamela hadn't been very successful, and he knew it was all his fault. Pamela had been just as sweet and as beautiful as she had been on their date Thursday night. It was Bruce who had been different this time.

He had sat across the table from her at the Box Tree Café, trying to listen to her gorgeous, lilting voice. But he couldn't stop going over in his mind the remarks people had been making about her.

He thought of the kids outside Big Mesa

High School, the week before he'd met Pamela. He remembered the looks of disdain on the girls' faces. "I'm looking for her," he had said. *"Isn't everyone?"* asked the fat, red-headed one. The tall boy had grinned lasciviously. *"If you find her, buddy, let me know!"* he had drawled.

Even Bruce's cousin Roger had warned him off her. *"There may be some things you don't know about her,"* he said.

By themselves, remarks like those didn't mean much, Bruce told himself. Pamela was beautiful. Plain girls like those two at Big Mesa had every reason to hate her. And the tall boy's comment was just the average, tasteless, locker-room kind of remark that all guys made about girls as good-looking as Pamela.

And jealousy could be the motive behind Roger's warning. Bruce had to admit that that wasn't Roger's usual reaction, though. He had probably just been showing some genuine concern about Bruce jumping so quickly into a serious romance.

But what about Amy Sutton? There was no mistaking her meaning in the school cafeteria Friday. She had been downright insulting.

Bruce had sat across the table from Pamela

that night, trying to reconcile this lovely, sweet girl with the words that kept going through his mind. *"Everybody knows Pamela—if you know what I mean!"* Amy had said with a wink. *"She's a very giving person."*

He had wanted to question Pamela, to find out about her past, but he couldn't come up with a tactful way to do it. Instead, he had sat there for two hours on their date that evening, looking at Pamela but hearing the voices of her detractors. That perfect girl couldn't be the same Pamela Robertson that Amy had criticized. But why would Amy lie to him about something like that?

He sat up in bed and punched his pillow decisively. Amy Sutton was a silly gossip, he reminded himself. Why was he letting her stupid comments get in the way of true love? She was probably just jealous, like the rest of them. Bruce knew he was the best catch at Sweet Valley High. And he and Amy had dated for a while. It probably made her furious to learn he was going out with an outsider.

Besides, he realized suddenly, Amy's relationship with Barry Rork seemed a little shaky. He hadn't thought about it before, but they had hardly said a word to each other throughout lunch. That was it, he decided. Amy had had a fight with her boyfriend, and now she couldn't stand to see two people who were truly happy together.

He smiled. He was a jerk for having listened to any of them. Pamela was still the girl of his dreams.

Then he sighed and slapped himself on the forehead. "I'm such an idiot!" he said aloud.

He had really screwed up their date that night. He'd been so preoccupied and confused that he barely paid attention to Pamela. She had been so understanding. She hadn't even seemed angry when Bruce took her home early, claiming to have a headache—just concerned about him.

Well, Bruce was going to make it up to her—and fast. First thing in the morning, he would show up on her doorstep with a picnic basket full of the finest pastries, fresh fruit, and imported cheese. Then they would drive out to the beach for a romantic, early-morning picnic.

It would be a glorious morning. The sun would sparkle off the waves, the sea gulls would be calling to one another, and a slow jazz song would be playing on his portable CD player.

He would watch as Pamela carefully broke apart a flaky croissant, then buttered it. She would hold it out to him, but he would set it down and take her in his arms. . . .

For the rest of that night, Bruce dreamed of Pamela, with sunshine creating highlights in her shiny black hair.

The next morning, Bruce stood on the doorstep of Pamela's modern, ranch-style house in Big Mesa. In his left hand he held a dozen long-stemmed roses wrapped in florist paper and ribbons. He raised his other hand to ring the doorbell, then stopped when a car roared up behind him.

Bruce spun around as a gold Trans Am screeched to a stop in front of the house. Pamela got out of the car. Her clothes were disheveled and her hair in disarray. The driver, a guy who looked a couple years older than Bruce, called roughly to her, but Bruce couldn't make out his words.

In the next instant the boy threw open his door, raced around the front of the car, and grabbed Pamela's arm. Bruce watched as the guy swung Pamela around to face him, watched as the guy roughly grabbed her other arm and pulled her to him. And Bruce watched as Pamela's head tilted back, as the guy put his lips on hers, as they held the kiss for what seemed an eternity.

Finally the guy released Pamela, and without so much as a parting word, stalked back to his car. A moment later, the car roared off. Bruce clutched the roses tightly as he watched Pamela approach the house. Suddenly her shoulders sagged, and he knew she had seen him. She trudged up the driveway toward him, an expression of weariness and sorrow on her beautiful face.

"Let me explain," she said softly.

"There's nothing to explain," he replied, looking down at her sadly from the front stoop.

She straightened, and he noticed determination in her huge blue eyes. "Oh yes there is," she said. "There's a lot you don't know about me."

"I know everything I need to know," Bruce responded grimly. As he said it, he remembered using those same words a few days earlier, when Roger had warned him that he didn't know enough about Pamela. *I know everything I need to know.*

Pamela shook her head in desperation. "No, Bruce," she said. "You don't know everything. You don't know that since meeting you I've changed. You don't know that I feel loved for the first time ever. You don't know that—"

"I don't want to hear it!" cried Bruce. He flung the roses at her feet and pushed past her.

"Wait, Bruce!" she called, stumbling. "Please! His name is Bobby. I was saying good-bye to him. I was telling him I couldn't see him again, but he gave me a hard time. He didn't want to let me go. You've got to believe me, Bruce!"

Bruce stomped across the yard to the black Porsche, climbed in, and slammed the door.

"Bruce, I love you!" Pamela cried, sobbing.

As the car roared away, Bruce caught sight of Pamela in his rearview mirror. She was standing alone in the yard, with a battered bouquet of roses at her feet.

"You're kidding!" Nicholas said to Olivia over Sunday brunch at Café Feliz. "The whole fund-raiser was a phony?"

"That's right," said Olivia. "But he really did buy my painting!"

Nicholas whistled and shook his head. "It's incredible that this Harry character would go to all that trouble to talk to you, when he could have just stopped you after class any Tuesday night. I admire his imagination—and his taste in women!"

"Thanks, Nicholas," Olivia said, smiling. "You know, I was really mad at him at first, but he was so sweet and shy, and he has such a terrific sense of humor. He managed to change my mind in a hurry!"

"So you were won over?" Nicholas said gleefully. "Do you *really* like him, Olivia?"

"Yeah," said Olivia with a sheepish grin. "I really like him. Nicholas, I was amazed at how quickly we hit it off. He loves art, of course, but he also loves poetry. And he's not a bad artist himself, though he's more interested in making a career doing museum or gallery work than actually painting."

She laughed. "And call me materialistic, but I certainly don't mind the fact that he's cute and rich, too!"

"So you've forgiven him for tricking you, and you've fallen madly in love."

"That's about it," said Olivia, nodding. "Though I can't believe I'm using the L word after only one evening of talking with a guy."

"You didn't use it," said Nicholas. "I did. But if the shoe fits—"

"OK, OK," Olivia agreed, laughing. "I admit it. I'm in love!"

"Good," said Nicholas. "It couldn't happen to a more deserving person—except maybe *me*."

Olivia sipped her coffee. "You're next," she said thoughtfully. "We're going to find a way for you to meet someone wonderful—I just haven't quite figured out how."

"I wouldn't even care if it was a really bizarre way, like you and Harry," Nicholas said.

"I'll let you know if I come up with anything," Olivia promised. She glanced at her watch. "Oops! I hate to break this up, but didn't you say you were meeting your father at noon to swab the decks, or whatever it is you do to a sailboat?"

"Gee, you're right!" said Nicholas, jumping to his feet. "And I'm late. Sorry to eat and run." He reached for his wallet. "Let me cover the bill."

"Don't you dare!" Olivia reprimanded him. "I told you this one's on me. Remember—I'm a thousand dollars richer!"

"That'll buy an awful lot of eggs benedict!" said Nicholas. "OK. It's a pleasure to be taken out by a beautiful young artist, even if she *is* in love with another man!" He feigned sorrow.

"Are we still on for cappuccino Wednesday?"

"You bet. And you can tell me all about seeing Harry in class on Tuesday."

After he left, Olivia pulled out the morning paper and settled back in her chair to finish her coffee.

"What's this?" she asked a few minutes later, sitting up straight. An advertisement had caught her eye: "Wanted—active, interesting singles, ages 18 to 25, to be contestants on *Hunks*, a new, national television dating show, taped in Los Angeles."

A slow smile spread across her face. "That's it!" she said aloud.

Nicholas had said he wouldn't mind a bizarre way of meeting someone; national television certainly qualified as bizarre. It was a weird idea, but maybe it would work, she decided. Sitting around in Sweet Valley certainly wasn't getting him anywhere. Olivia scanned the ad again. Nicholas certainly met all the requirements.

She tore the ad from the paper, put it in her shoulder bag, and asked the waiter for the check.

"Liz, I've got to go back to school soon. Can I talk to you a minute?" came her brother's voice at her bedroom door.

Elizabeth looked up from the book she had been trying to read. She still didn't feel like talking, but Steven was trying so hard to be helpful that she didn't have the heart to turn him away.

"Sure, Steven," she said. "But I can't promise that I'll be very good company. You know, I've been staring at the same page for fifteen minutes and still haven't the foggiest idea of what it says."

"You're doing fine, Liz," he said gently, pushing the door open. He walked in and sat next to her on the bed. "Nobody expects you to be the life of the party right now. But you might feel better if you talked about it."

"Maybe," she said. "But I honestly don't know what there is to say."

"Just tell me what's on your mind," he urged. "I'm a pretty understanding guy."

"You are, Steven. I don't know what I'd do without you and Mom and Dad and Enid—" She turned away, biting her lip, and stared at the door that led through the bathroom to her sister's room. Steven followed her gaze.

He put his hand on hers. "I know," he said. "Jessica's being pretty rough on you. But you've got to understand what she's going through. You've got to realize that it will take some time—"

"That's what Mom and Enid said," Elizabeth acknowledged. "What nobody seems to understand is that Jessica is *right*. And time isn't going to change that, Steve. No matter how hard it is, I've got to accept the fact that Jess and I will never be close again."

Steve shook his head. "No, Liz. I think you're wrong," he said. "And it scares me that you'd even think such a thing. You sound as if you've given up too."

"Too?" Elizabeth asked. "Who else have you talked with? Did Jessica say something?"

"No," said Steven. "I meant Mom and Dad. Jessica hardly says a word to me. But all four of you are acting as if you're giving up, as if the situation is hopeless. It scares me."

"But Steven, the situation *is* hopeless," Elizabeth said quietly. "Sam is dead, and nothing I can do will change that."

"But *you're* still alive," Steven reminded her. "And so is Jessica. It's terrible that Sam's life had to end like that. But you sound as if yours is over too."

"Sam's life didn't just *end*," she answered slowly, looking him straight in the eyes. She pointed to herself for emphasis. "*I killed him!* Now I have to face the consequences of that."

"Stop beating yourself up—"

"Ever since the accident, I've had an awful feeling that it's not over. Steven, things will get worse; I know they will. The other shoe is going to fall—and soon."

"You're getting carried away with guilt, Liz," Steven said quietly. "But someday you'll realize that you're not to blame."

Elizabeth shook her head.

"I think you're right about one thing," he said sadly. "Things *are* going to get worse. This family has fallen apart, and I don't know how to help put it back together."

He wrapped his arms around her and held her tightly for a moment. Then he stood. "You

193

know, I'm almost afraid to go back to school and leave you here."

"Thanks, Steven," Elizabeth said, almost in a whisper. "But there's nothing you can do to change anything."

Steven nodded sadly and headed for the door. He opened it and started to walk into the hallway, then turned back toward her. His brown eyes looked wistful, as if he thought he wouldn't be seeing her again for a long, long time.

"Liz, I know it's hard, but please stop worrying that the worst is yet to come," he said. He sounded as if he was trying to convince himself as much as her.

A few minutes later Elizabeth heard the kitchen door slam as her brother left to return to school. As the sound echoed through the house, she felt a sinking sensation in the pit of her stomach.

From the railroad tracks on the outskirts of town came the roar of a freight train rushing by.

Chapter 12

Jessica, sitting in her room, had overheard the last part of Steven's sentence in the hallway outside a half hour earlier: ". . . *the worst is yet to come.*"

How could things get worse? she wondered. Sam was dead—gone forever. And as for Elizabeth—

No, Jessica told herself. *Don't think about Liz.* Elizabeth had been driving the Jeep that night. What happened before they got in the car didn't make any difference. It was Elizabeth who killed him.

Restless, Jessica walked out of her room and went downstairs to the living room. She turned on the stereo, and the loud driving beat of a rock song filled the room. She hoped it would drown out the sound of her own thoughts. She threw herself on the couch and stared at the ceiling.

"Jessica?" her mother's voice cut through the music a few minutes later. "Are you in the living room? I thought I heard someone at the door."

Jessica turned down the radio. Someone was insistently ringing the doorbell.

Jessica shivered as a wave of irrational fear washed over her. She shook it off, rose from the couch, and headed toward the door. She turned the stereo off as she passed it, but the sudden silence seemed even louder than the rock music.

Jessica opened the door and jumped as if she had been struck. Standing in the door-way were two blue-uniformed police officers. Jessica grabbed hold of the door and froze.

"Jessica, who was that at the—" her mother began, walking into the hallway behind her.

"Mrs. Wakefield?" said the taller of the two officers. "I'm Detective Roger Marsh"—

he gestured toward the other policeman—
"and this is Detective Andrew Perez."
Detective Marsh looked at Jessica, who was
still frozen in place, clutching the door. "May
we come in?"

Alice Wakefield gently pulled Jessica's arm
away from the door and opened it wider. "Of
course," she said, flustered. She motioned the
officers toward the living room. "Please come
in. I'll call my husband." The officers sat down
on the couch.

"Ned!" she called down the hall. Mr.
Wakefield was in his study. "Elizabeth!"

Jessica gulped and sat down quickly in a
chair across from the couch. She was shaking
so badly that she felt if she didn't sit, her legs
would give out. Her mind seemed to be racing
all over the place. She couldn't control her
thoughts any more than she could control the
shaking of her body.

"Can I get you a cup of coffee, or a soft
drink?" Mrs. Wakefield asked the police officers.

For a moment, Jessica wondered how her
mother could sound so controlled. Then she
realized that there was a note of sheer panic
in Alice Wakefield's voice. *Of course Mom's*

afraid, Jessica thought. *One of her daughters is about to get arrested.*

Then she remembered that her mother had no idea of Jessica's part in the accident. Her parents would be so disappointed in her when they found out. The thought of their reaction when they heard the truth about Jessica was almost as bad as the idea of going to jail.

And they were probably going to find out any minute now, Jessica thought. *The police must know it was me. They must know everything.*

Mr. Wakefield and Elizabeth reached the living room at the same time. Elizabeth's face went white when she saw the police uniforms. For a moment Jessica thought her sister would pass out.

The twins' mother motioned around the room. "This is my husband, Ned, and my daughters, Jessica and Elizabeth," she said to the detectives. Her voice was calm and completely flat.

The police officers introduced themselves. Elizabeth had remained standing, and now her father put his hand on her shoulder and directed her to sit down.

Jessica noticed that her sister moved slowly, as if she were heading toward a firing squad. Though Elizabeth seemed scared, Jessica was surprised to see that she also looked resigned, and even a little relieved. She sat down, and her father sat next to her. Mrs. Wakefield perched on the edge of an easy chair.

But Jessica couldn't help wondering if *she* was the one they were after, not Elizabeth. It was illegal to give alcohol to a minor. Maybe somebody had seen her spiking her sister's drink. Maybe somebody knew what had really happened that night.

"Mr. and Mrs. Wakefield," Detective Marsh was saying. "We have some questions to ask your daughter, about a Saturday night three weeks ago—"

"The night of the prom at Sweet Valley High," Sergeant Hadley concluded impatiently.

Detective Marsh was about forty, Jessica decided. He was lanky, with dark, thinning hair and a kind voice. The other officer was older—a stocky, powerful-looking man with a scowl on his face.

I can't believe I'm about to be arrested and

I'm just sitting here, casually sizing up what the police officers look like, she thought. But Jessica knew there was nothing casual about what she was feeling. Grasping onto concrete details was the only thing that might keep her from going to pieces.

Jessica took a deep breath and was about to speak.

"Which girl is Elizabeth?" Sergeant Hadley asked abruptly, looking from twin to twin.

Jessica let out a long sigh. She wasn't the one they were looking for, after all. They didn't know it was her fault!

Then the officer's words hit her like a blow to the chest: *They were after Elizabeth.*

"I'm Elizabeth," her sister volunteered. She sounded calm, but Jessica saw that she was clenching her hands together so tightly that they appeared bloodless.

"Were you aware that your blood alcohol level was well above the legal limit that night?" Detective Perez asked sharply.

Jessica saw her mother's face turn as pale as Elizabeth's.

"I don't think it's wise for my daughter to answer questions like this without an attorney present," Ned Wakefield said.

"No, Daddy," Elizabeth objected. "Don't try to protect me. I'll tell them the truth about what I know." She lowered her voice, almost to a whisper. "But I'm afraid I don't know much," she added.

"Elizabeth," began Detective Marsh. "Hospital records show that you and Sam Woodruff—both minors—tested very high for blood alcohol immediately after the accident. You were obviously drinking at the dance. Did you bring the liquor to school with you that night, or did somebody give it to you there?"

Jessica sat rigidly on the edge of her chair, waiting for her sister's answer.

Elizabeth shook her head, totally bewildered. "I don't know what you're talking about," she said, her eyes filling with tears. "I don't even drink."

"Elizabeth, the test doesn't lie," Detective Perez said.

Elizabeth looked so despondent that Jessica found herself feeling sorry for her.

"Miss Wakefield," Detective Perez began. "A seventeen-year-old boy was killed in that accident. This is a serious situation, and I won't have you playing games with us. Just answer the questions as they're put to

201

you. Where did you get the booze?"

Jessica felt panicked. *I should tell them the truth*, she realized. *I should tell them where Elizabeth got the alcohol. She could get into terrible trouble, and I'm the only one who can keep her out of it.*

"I'm sorry, Detective," Elizabeth said. "I don't mean to be difficult. I honestly don't remember much at all about that night. I don't remember drinking, and I don't even know how the accident happened."

"I find that hard to believe, Miss Wakefield," said Detective Perez, with a frown on his face.

"Detective," Mr. Wakefield said seriously, "Elizabeth has never been involved in any sort of trouble. If she says she doesn't remember, then she doesn't remember."

Suddenly Jessica was annoyed. Her parents were always bragging about how Elizabeth never got into any trouble. If it had been Jessica being questioned, she was sure her father wouldn't have been so quick to defend *her* honesty.

"We're not doubting your daughter's honesty, Mr. Wakefield," said Detective Marsh, with a sidelong glance at his colleague. "But she's young and frightened, and she's been through a traumatic experience. Perhaps she just hasn't thought about it hard enough."

He gave Elizabeth a kind smile. "Elizabeth," he said, "we really need you to tell us. Think carefully and try to remember. You certainly aren't the first high-school kids in town to take a few drinks at a party. You're minors, and giving alcohol to minors is a crime, so we *do* need to know who provided the alcohol that you and Sam Woodruff were drinking that night. Did Sam bring it?"

"No!" said Elizabeth emphatically. "Well, I guess I don't know that for sure," she admitted. "But I certainly didn't see him with any alcohol. And I do know—I mean, I *did* know Sam. I know he would never bring liquor to a school dance."

Detective Perez threw up his hands. "This is getting us nowhere," he said, glaring at Elizabeth. His face was turning red.

Jessica opened her mouth to speak, but the sergeant fired another question at Elizabeth first.

"Was it you who was driving the Jeep when you left the dance that night with Sam Woodruff?"

Elizabeth left the dance with Sam, Jessica remembered. How could her sister have done that to her? How could Elizabeth steal her boyfriend away from her like that—twice? First she drove away with him, and then she killed him. It just wasn't fair, Jessica thought glumly. It just wasn't fair.

"I—I don't know if I was driving," said Elizabeth. "I don't remember."

"Don't answer too quickly," said Detective Marsh in a soothing voice. "Think about it carefully. Who was driving the Jeep that was involved in the accident?"

"I'm sorry," Elizabeth repeated. "I've done nothing *but* think about it carefully for three weeks. And I still don't remember. I don't know who was driving. In fact, as I said before, I don't remember anything about the accident."

"Elizabeth," said Detective Marsh, "we're trying to be patient with you, but you've already been given a lot more breaks than you know about. Normally, in a case like this, we would have pulled you in for questioning weeks ago."

"Frankly, I've been wondering why you didn't," Ned Wakefield admitted.

"Actually, it was because of you, sir," answered the tall, thin officer. "We know that you're a prominent member of the local legal community. A lot of people in the district attorney's office think very highly of you. Because of your position, because of Elizabeth's age, and because she's an honor student with no record of any trouble, we were asked to take special care with this investigation." He looked pointedly at Elizabeth. "We've tried to give her every benefit of the doubt."

"We appreciate that," said Mr. Wakefield. "But what happens next?"

Detective Marsh ran a hand through his sparse hair. "That depends," he said.

"It depends on whether your daughter cooperates with us and answers the questions truthfully," broke in Detective Perez.

"I *am* answering them truthfully," Elizabeth insisted, chin held high. She looked so brave, Jessica thought. *Why is Elizabeth always the brave one?*

"I'd give *anything* to be able to tell you about the last half of that evening, Detective," Elizabeth continued. "But you have to believe me when I tell you that I simply don't remember it."

Both officers rose to their feet. A feeling of dread gripped Jessica, and she could see in her sister's face that Elizabeth felt it too.

"Whether you remember or not, it was *your* car," said Detective Marsh. "And, from evidence found at the scene of the accident— as well as from the location of the young man's body on the road—we've determined that it was you, and not Sam Woodruff, who was driving that night. Elizabeth Wakefield, you are under arrest for involuntary manslaughter."

Mr. and Mrs. Wakefield both gasped.

Then he read her her rights.

Elizabeth obediently rose to her feet. Jessica thought the officers looked surprised at how composed Elizabeth seemed. But Jessica knew her sister well enough to recognize the terror in her eyes.

Jessica stood up at the same time. It wasn't too late, she thought. She could still tell them the truth about that night. *Elizabeth didn't know about the alcohol,* she wanted to blurt out. *I spiked her drink. It was me! It was all my fault!*

Her parents rose slowly and stood on either side of Elizabeth. Each of them raised a hand and placed it on their daughter's shoulders, and Jessica could see the love in their eyes.

She imagined how they would feel about her, Jessica, if she told them the truth. What would they think of a girl who would get her own twin sister drunk—and then allow her to go through the last three, horrible weeks, without stepping forward and taking the blame for her own boyfriend's death?

They wouldn't stand there like that with their arms around me *if they knew the truth,* she told herself. *And I wouldn't deserve it.*

"Do you realize what you're doing?" Detective Marsh asked. Jessica looked up, startled. Did he know the truth, after all? Then she sighed with relief. *No,* she realized. It was Elizabeth he was speaking to, not her.

"What do you mean, Detective?" Elizabeth asked uncertainly.

"We've done enough of a background check on you to know that you've always been a good kid," he said seriously. "But we can't protect you if you won't tell us the truth. Your entire future could be at stake here, Elizabeth. Do you really want to go on trial for the death of your boyfriend?"

Jessica stiffened. "Sam was *my*

boyfriend—not hers!" she objected. Jessica sat back down in the chair, and tears ran down her face as she addressed her sister. "Sam—was—my—boyfriend," she said between sobs.

The officers looked around the room uncomfortably. Then Detective Marsh spoke. "You'll have to come down to the police station with us now."

"Is it really necessary to bring Elizabeth downtown?" Mr. Wakefield asked after a moment.

"Only for booking," answered Detective Marsh. "I'm sure she'll be released into your custody as soon as a trial date is set." He paused for a moment. "If you'd rather drive your own car with your daughter, we can follow you in the squad car. It's not police procedure, but I think we can trust you."

Detective Perez looked as if he was about to object, but the tall officer silenced him with a gesture.

"Thank you," Ned answered quietly. "I'll go with her, Alice. You'd better stay here with Jessica."

Mrs. Wakefield nodded grimly and then hugged Elizabeth, but Elizabeth's eyes never left her sister's face. When her father led her out the door a few minutes later, she was still staring back at Jessica.

"I'm sorry," Elizabeth mouthed silently. Her eyes were full of love and regret. Then the door closed.

Margo stood alone the next evening, looking out the window of her boxlike room at the Y. The sky outside was dark gray, lit by a few streaks of flame from the fading sunset. Behind her on the night table was a paycheck and a ruby ring.

She turned around, sat on the bed, and picked up the ring. As she fingered it, a sly smile played at the corners of her mouth. It had been almost too easy, she thought. That phony story about her dead mother and her kind sister had done the trick. Ms. Rossi had felt so sorry for her that she'd paid her for her first week in advance!

"Now don't refuse to take this money, Michelle," the woman had said, folding the check into Margo's hand as if she were as young as Georgie. "I know you need it now—not next week—to pay for your books and to help out your sister."

Margo had stifled a laugh as the woman gave her a quick hug.

"Goodness knows I never pay for anything in advance," Ms. Rossi confided. "It just isn't good business sense. But this is different. You and I are kindred spirits, I can tell. And I know that you're going to work out just fine as Georgie's baby-sitter."

That "kindred spirits" remark had almost done it. Margo had come close to telling the deluded twit just what she really thought of her.

Instead, Margo had thanked her sweetly and said an affectionate, but insincere, good-bye to the little red-haired brat. Then she picked up her shoulder bag to leave for the day, thinking of the expensive ruby ring she had slipped into it while Georgie watched cartoons on television.

Every little bit helps, said the raspy voice inside her head.

"That's for sure," Margo answered aloud. "It would take me years to get west if I had to rely on what that cheapskate is paying me."

She had her "savings," of course, but she wasn't fooling herself. You could never have too much money—especially if you had a plan to carry out. She knew it would take time to determine her destination, make her way there, and then set up a new life for herself. Money would give her the time she needed to make sure everything worked out exactly right.

Meanwhile, even the baby-sitting wasn't turning out to be too bad, Margo decided. Georgie was OK for a little kid. He was quiet and didn't make too many demands on her— she'd made sure of that from the start. As soon as his mother had left, Margo sat down in front of the boy and stared at him. She hadn't said a word. She had just stared at him for a full ten minutes, with what Nina used to call "that mean look."

That shut the kid up, all right, she thought with a chuckle. Georgie was basically a wimp, and now he was terrified of her. Margo was sure she would have no trouble with him.

As for his older brother, Margo wouldn't mind getting *into* a little trouble with him. She had met Josh that day, and he was even better-looking in person than in the photo. He'd been wearing supertight jeans and had his hair slicked back. Margo licked her lips, thinking about him.

No, she told herself, rising from the bed. She walked back to the window and looked out at the darkening sky. She didn't have time for fooling around. She had to concentrate on making money. Also, she needed to keep moving. She didn't need anything or anyone to tie me her down.

The pounding was starting up again in Margo's head. She looked out the window at the dingy neighborhood. *Cleveland!* she thought with a snort of derision. *This is no better than Long Island. But at least I have a purpose here. I'm on my way.*

Yes. She would steer clear of Josh Rossi and not make any attachments in Cleveland. Besides, in all of her sixteen years, nobody had ever really cared for her. Why would Josh be any different?

"I don't need him!" she said fervently, staring out the window. "I don't need anybody."

In the distance, a train whistle sounded. With it, Margo's destination came to her.

California, the voice said inside her head. *California.*

As soon as she heard the voice, Margo realized that she had known it all along. She would go to California, where a new life would be waiting for her. She would go to Southern California—she had heard it was warm and sunny there, and the ocean waves tumbled and roared against shining white beaches.

Margo stood at the window for a long time, but the scene she saw outside was nowhere near Cleveland.

A new life was waiting for her, somewhere out there, somewhere in California.

☎

1 (800) I LUV BKS!

If you'd like to hear more about your
favorite young adult novels and writers . . .
OR
If you'd like to tell us what you thought
of this book or other books
you've recently read . . .

CALL US at 1(800) I LUV BKS
[1(800)458-8257]

You'll hear a new message about books and
other interesting subjects each month.

**The call is free to you, but please get
your parents' permission first.**

MURDER AND MYSTERY STRIKES

America's favorite teen series has a hot line of
Super Thrillers! ®

It's super excitement, super suspense, and super thrills as Jessica and Elizabeth Wakefield put on their detective caps in the SWEET VALLEY HIGH SUPER THRILLERS! Follow these two sleuths as they witness a murder...find themselves running from the mob...and uncover the dark secrets of a mysterious woman. SWEET VALLEY HIGH SUPER THRILLERS are guaranteed to keep you on the edge of your seat!

YOU'LL WANT TO READ THEM ALL!

❏ #1: DOUBLE JEOPARDY   26905-4/$3.50
❏ #2: ON THE RUN   27230-6/$3.50
❏ #3: NO PLACE TO HIDE   27554-2/$3.50
❏ #4: DEADLY SUMMER   28010-4/$3.50
❏ #5: MURDER ON THE LINE   29308-7/$3.50

HAVE YOU READ THE LATEST SWEET VALLEY SUPER STARS

❏ #1: LILA'S STORY   28296-4/$3.50
❏ #2: BRUCE'S STORY   28464-9/$3.50
❏ #3: ENID'S STORY   28576-9/$3.50
❏ #4: OLIVIA'S STORY   29359-1/$3.50
❏ #5: TODD'S STORY   29207-2 /$3.50

The most exciting stories ever in Sweet Valley history...

FRANCINE PASCAL'S

☐ **THE WAKEFIELDS OF SWEET VALLEY**
Sweet Valley Saga #1
$3.99/$4.99 in Canada   29278-1
Following the lives, loves and adventures of five
generations of young women who were Elizabeth and
Jessica's ancestors, The Wakefields of Sweet Valley
begins in 1860 when Alice Larson, a 16-year-old
Swedish girl, sails to America.

☐ **THE WAKEFIELD LEGACY: The Untold Story**
Sweet Valley Saga #2
$3.99/$4.99 In Canada   29794-5
Chronicling the lives of Jessica and Elizabeth's
father's ancestors, The Wakefield Legacy begins with
Lord Theodore who crosses the Atlantic and falls in
love with Alice Larson.